MW01074746

AN ANTHOLOGY OF MOVIE THEATER HORROR

CINEMA VISCERA

EDITED BY SAM RICHARD

CONTENTS

INTRODUCTION

SAM RICHARD

The Blob, Demons, An American Werewolf in London, Gremlins, Popcorn, the list goes on and on. Horror movies set in, or partially in, movie theaters goes back damn near as far as the genre. Something about the possibility of skulking maniacs with knives, or small creatures, or ecological terrors to be waiting in the darkness of a movie theater just begs to be explored. Something about shared horrors on screen potentially spilling out into the real world. It's all perfect fodder for horror—both film and fiction.

And it's a micro-genre I absolutely love.

So I asked some friends to help me make an anthology on the loose theme of horror in—or involving—movie theaters. It didn't have to be traditional. They could do drive-ins, microcinemas, backyard DIY illegal showings of cult movies. It didn't matter. I just wanted the blood on the page to splash onto the big screen, at least a little bit.

Jo Quenell, Katy Michelle Quinn, and I have a history of doing this. First the three of us did *Lazermall* (published by our friend Ira Rat at Filthy Loot), and then with *Beautiful/Grotesque*, where I asked the two of them and two other friends (Joanna Koch and Roland Blackburn) to loosely use the concept of 'where the beautiful and the grotesque collide' and an illustration by Zdzisław Beksiński as a guidepost from which to write some weird horror. Now the three of us are back, this time joined by two of our other good friends and fantastic writers: Charles Austin Muir and Brendan Vidito.

It is my hope that these weird ideas can be launching points for great works of horror fiction; and so far that has worked out well. What I didn't expect was for this book to be as dark as it is. As fucked up. As full of pain and *viscera*. Naively, I seriously assumed we'd all write fun pieces capturing that 80s VHS vibe. What we all wrote—well—it's different than that.

This book is uncomfortable, harsh, disturbing. Basically, content-warnings abound (detailed further in the Content Warnings section). Everyone spilled serious blood to make these stories. It soaked into the ink, becoming part of the book. These stories hold our anxieties and fears, our realities and lives, our hearts and our souls.

So thank you for reading it. For supporting Weirdpunk, the writers, and the work that we do.

Thank you to Katy, Jo, Charles, and Brendan, not only for being into this idea, but for also writing your hearts out. Thanks for trusting me with your work and for your patience, as this took longer to come out than initially discussed.

Thank you to Amy M. Vaughn for coming up with the perfect title for this anthology. And everyone else who offered suggestion when I was stuck on some dumb bullshit.

Finally, with a shattered heart, I need to thank best friend and closest companion who died suddenly during the last legs of making this book. Nero, you were the best pup, the mightiest emperor, and you will never be forgotten. Thanks for being there for me during everything, and for keeping me alive after Mo died. I know you'll always be by my side, I'm just sorry I can't see you anymore.

THE WATCHER'S DIGEST
KATY MICHELLE QUINN

"SO WHAT SHE'S A SWAPPER," the silver-suited man says. "It's just a fuck. Give me a sec."

Kyra leans quietly against a filthy carpeted wall, waiting for the man who had just paid her to come get his money's worth. She looks around. The ruin is dead of light, a stark contrast from Cascadia, the neon-veined citystate her and the other Scroungers inhabit. She blinks, activating a retinal implant that increases the aperture of her iris beyond natural limits. Light floods her brain, giving her the ability to make out more of the room. A coliseum of plastic-backed chairs, pockmarked with gaps to rival the smile of a Scrounger. Those that weren't consumed by time and vermin still sport what looks like scraps of cotton-based fabric. A rarity in these days. She'll have to bring the crew here when she's off-shift. That Scrap gotta be worth a decent trade.

She clears her throat and puts on her best fuck-me smile, the unbroken thing that gets her work even more than her subtle curves.

"I don't have all day, hun!" she sings.

"One sec!" the grunted reply, before the man again addresses his comrade. "Just keep watch. Like ten minutes max. I'll be quick."

Another man sighs, a raspy sound enhanced by a vocal chip. Must be a veteran.

Kyra utters something of her own and returns her attention to the half-ripped screen that spans the ruined theater before her. At least, she thinks that's what they were called. *Theaters*. Gathering spaces where groups of strangers would convene to watch vids adjacently. A weird, outdated concept. These days, there isn't a clip around that can't be streamed to your home holoscreen, were you lucky enough to have one. Kyra wasn't.

The silence is eerie, too. Stale. She doesn't wanna be here longer than she has to. She blinks again, and her field of vision display goes blue as the pulse reader activates. Just to ensure they don't have company. Empty navy spans the room in front of her, interrupted only by the emanating waves of her own heartbeat. To her right, the two men's pulses blink rapidly, a sign of stress, pleasure, exertion, or all three. One blinking waveform begins moving towards Kyra, and she blinks the display back to lowlight.

Finally.

The silver-suited man approaches, hands already fumbling at his pants.

"Sorry," he says. "Rocco was being a pussy."

Kyra rolls her eyes imperceptibly.

"What's with this place, anyway?" she asks as the man pushes his waistband to his knees. "There are closer spots."

The man chuckles like a child.

"I worry I'll get walked in on," he tells her. "Could be dangerous for someone in my position to be seen with, you know. Someone like you."

I'll *get walked in on.* As if he's alone in the act, and she's nothing but a service droid.

"Weird room," she comments.

"Yeah," the man says, scoffing. "'Movie theaters.'"

He walks closer and leans back on the carpeted wall, gesturing at the tube of flesh rising from his crotch. Kyra gets down on her knees and wraps her fingers around it. Impressive, how her small hands could so totally eclipse a member. She squeezes until she feels the pulse quicken in his veins.

"I thought that's what they were called," she tells him. "People watched vids together, right?"

His dick stiffens in her grip, the tip poking out of her fist like a turtle from its shell. She takes a tongue to it, and the man groans a moment before regaining composure.

"Uh huh," the man says. "Strange concept. People that didn't know each other or anything, uh, just sat here together and, mmm, watched vids."

Kyra makes a ring of her forefinger and thumb, slides it down his shaft as she takes it into her mouth. The microimplants her skin is equipped with warm as if with natural excitement.

"They were around for a few decades," the man continues. Kyra pauses before realizing he's still talking about theaters. "Maybe close to a century. Twentieth, twenty-first. Something like that."

Kyra does her best to stifle a laugh, which is easier done with a cock in her mouth. It's amazing the things people will ramble about when a sex worker goes down on them. It's something you quickly learn: that everyone has something weird that excites them. Even if it isn't sexual, it often comes out during the act.

"Mhmm," Kyra says with a full mouth. She makes the sound as sexy as she can while still showing him that she's listening to his lecture.

"They fell out of use during the Distance Disease, I think," he punctuates the thought with a moan. "Never really came back. Most of 'em got bought out and destroyed, but a few survived the century. Guess this is one, ah, fuck yeah, keep going."

Kyra slips her mouth off him.

"On, not in," she tells him.

The man rolls his eyes and begins jacking at his saliva-soaked sex. With the other hand, he grabs Kyra's hair and pulls her face into his crotch. He smells like sweet urine and onions.

"I grew up near here," the man says, grunting. "This place always, ah, fuck, always, uh, intrigued…."

His syllables are overtaken by the sound of effort and cussing, and he splashes up onto Kyra's face. His cum shoots out in spurts, decorating her skin with cream-colored globs. She wipes one out of her eye and smiles up at him.

"Finished?" she asks as if it isn't obvious.

The man nods, out of breath.

"Fuck," he exhales.

The smile instantly vanishes, and she stands up. She wipes the rest of his spunk off her face and flings it to the ground with a sickened shake.

"Okay, good," she says. "If you want to see me again next week, you know where I'll be. Next time be ready. I can't wait around like that."

She starts walking through the two-sided tunnel that serves as the theater's entrance.

"Thanks again," the man says, half-heartedly.

"Yeah," Kyra says without looking back. "Thanks for the cred. And the theater lesson."

She hears him chuckle as she pushes through the door.

The man's friend, Rocco, stands outside with a weird look on his face. He seems uncomfortable, whether with the locale or the paid sex she can't tell.

She wipes off smeared lipstick with a bare forearm.

"He'll be out in a sec," she tells Rocco, before vanishing towards the light at the entrance of the ruin.

———

KYRA BLINKS her time display on and off obsessively. Around her, the crew lounges in wait for their final member.

"Always fucking late," she mutters.

She's standing in front of the abandoned theater she'd sucked off Silver in earlier. It's dark now, darker than she's used to. The pinkish neon glow of Cascadia seems muted from this distance, though they couldn't be farther than a mile or two from the nearest edge. Even so, asphalt crumbles darkly before them, bent metal poles sprouting and drooping from it like dead vines. It makes her nervous. The lack of light, the lack of anything to hide behind. Anything but the theater, which with any luck would feed the lot of them for a few weeks.

"Dex, when did you last see them?" Kyra spits at her compatriot, a teal-haired enby defined more by their piercings than anything else.

Dex shrugs in response, leather-sleeved arms crossed over their chest in boredom. The minute vibrations of their irises tell Kyra that their either vidding or keeping fresh on the various Scrounger subthreads.

"They said they would be here."

Kyra blinks on her time display again, though it hasn't changed.

Besides Kyra and Dex, there's three others that make up their Scrounger crew. Mai and Kai, lanky twins distinguishable by contrasting green and pink hair, lean against the ragged wall of the theater nearby, waiting, like they all were, for Sprout. Sprout was what you might call the brains of the crew, the most educated though even they hadn't completed Basic Courses. But what they had in intelligence they lacked in punctuality, an ever-present thorn in Kyra's side.

As she curses Sprout for the second time, a dark speck materializes out of the distant dark, running and waving as if there wasn't danger hidden in every shadow. Kyra motions for them to stay small, something they finally do with a sheepish look. Hunched down in their oversized coat, they almost appear to be floating towards the group like a ghost.

"Sorry," Sprout mouths as they join the crew under what awning remains attached to the theater. They lean in and kiss Kyra, a move that gets them toe-in on her good side again.

"Always keeping me waiting," she says, waving the group to gather. "So I was here earlier, and I didn't see sign of anything then, but that was day. Everyone armed?"

Everyone nods except Sprout, who for reasons of constitution refuses to carry a weapon. As ever, Kyra would play rogue to their scholar. As if to punctuate her point, she yanks matching plasma-edged blades from the holsters on the back of her belt.

With a nod, she steps through the bent scrap that was once the theater's doors. The blue-edged blades glow singularly as she's surrounded by the darkness.

"C'mon," she hisses to the group.

As always, Kyra has to be the guts of the crew. Crunching steps say that her friends have answered her call, though after a moment of hesitation.

Sprout yelps a few feet behind her.

"What?" she spouts, spinning one-eighty, blades gripped tight.

Sprout stands on one foot, the other dripping translucent goo back into the puddle they had just stepped in.

"What is it?" they say, stuttering.

Kyra squats and blinks on her lowlight program. She sticks a finger into what looks like a large, pinkish amoeba. Its skin breaks like a crust, letting her feel the viscous innards. She pulls out and smells her finger, noticing only a faint sweetness.

"They used to sell snacks at these places," Mai whispers. "Maybe it's that?"

Mai was into historical infrastructure, a strange niche that had helped the Scroungers in more than a few instances. Though Kyra couldn't see her expression, she could hear the excitement bubbling in her voice.

"Maybe," Kyra says, unsure. To Sprout, "Scrape it off and let's go."

Sprout complies, the sound of their chunky-soled boots against the decrepit flooring echoing throughout the foyer.

Kyra leads the way to the first theater, twin doors marked by a barely visible 6. She pushes the door open, quickly scans for signs of life, and beckons the crew inside with a glowing blade. Mai and Kai each grip their own knives tighter, and Dex holds fast to his self-built pistol. She knows she's asking a lot, taking them here, but the payoff could be huge. Maybe they could even afford dinner bought from a restaurant once they sell the Scrap.

"I scanned," she assures them.

Hesitantly, the group enters the theater.

As the door shuts behind them, silence begins its rule. Dead buildings like these are always quiet, but this room especially so. Maybe due to the weather-stripped doors and the abundance of true fabric.

"It's all over the chairs, and I remember seeing some scraps on the floor," Kyra tells everyone. "Fan out and take as much as you can."

Their little crew disperses into the dark theater. Dex, Sprout, and Mai shine wrist-mounted lights in cones in front of them. Kai, the only other Swapper here, blinks through what must be her preferred visual settings. They begin tearing and cutting the fabric in anxious silence, stuffing the Scrap into whatever bags they brought with them. Sprout stuffs the abundant pockets of their coat, giving them the look of a bulbous rodent.

Kyra takes to the mezzanine, an area that the rest are avoiding. Maybe because it's a bit darker, a little more removed. Up to her to take action, yet again. She begins using her blades for their primary use, piecing apart Scrap like this seat fabric. While she plays the badass, the truth is she's only been in a few fights where she's bitten back. Being a sex worker and Swapper, there was much more benefit to keeping a cool head in stressful situations. Still, she kept the blades on her in case.

As she walks the final row of chairs, chopping fabric off to expose chunks of foam, Kyra sees what looks like a window in the middle of the back wall. She puts her face up to it, trying to see what's inside. Immediately across from her, a broken lens stares back. She looks back at the torn silverscreen before putting it together. It's a projection system. How archaic. Mai will love this. Kyra turns back to the window, intending to call Mai up here, but something she sees startles her to silence. She spots something beyond the darkened glass, a place where the black lightlessness glows with a pinkish hue before disappearing completely. Kyra blinks on her pulse reader reactively. Nothing. No sign of life until she turns around and watches her friends weaving through dilapidated rows of seating.

Kyra blinks the reader off.

She slinks down the mezzanine stairs, cursing her jumpiness in this new ruin.

"How's the Scrap?" she asks the room.

The crew respond with enthusiastic yelps, a victory in comparison to the asphalt-flat affects most Scroungers wore proudly.

"Ready to go in a bit?"

"Actually," Sprout says. "I was thinking we could stay the night. This place has more room and coverage than the encampment, and in the morning we'd have more energy for the haul back."

Sprout looks around, their buoyant expression a stark contrast to their overladen coat. The rest of the crew stay silent for a moment.

"It *is* nice and quiet," Dex finally says. "I could actually get some reading done."

Kyra sighs. In most circumstances, the group would never settle down for the night in a new place. It was just common sense. But they were usually scrounging in much more central areas, with much less Scrap. Hauling heaps all the way back to the city, then further to the encampment, would be a long, dangerous hike, and the clock was already nipping at the small hours.

"It's not like we're alone," Sprout says. "We can watch in turns."

They had a point. And being the most timid of the group, Sprout's endorsement of the idea made it seem much less risky.

"I'm in," Kyra says after a minute, "if we check the rest of the place first."

Sprout makes a victory fist. Dex, Mai, and Kai nod in their separate yet similarly lackadaisical ways.

"Sprout and I can check the back four auditoriums," Kyra says. "Do you three feel okay checking the right wing?"

"Sure," Dex says. They palm-slap their pistol as if to beat out any glitches.

"Back at the entrance in ten?" Mai asks.

Kai adds, "Then we can decide what we're going to do."

Kyra nods.

"Let's get going," she says. "I'm already tired."

———

ELEVEN MINUTES LATER, the group gathers in front of a crushed glass case, bits of broken plastic littering the area around their feet. It would be sticky if anything edible hadn't rotted away under 200 years of dust.

"We didn't see anything of concern," says Dex, ever the enunciator.

"Same," Sprout says. They clear their throat. "Should we?"

"There was a basement," Kyra inserts. "Makes me a little nervous, but I walked to the bottom of the stairs and pulse-scanned. Not even a skrat."

"So we're staying?" Mai asks, making jazz hands.

Kyra thinks they seem a little too excited, like a goth kid who haphazardly sleeps in a haunted house, but that's probably due to their interest in the building itself. She hopes it doesn't extend beyond that. Mai could be known to keep things hid longer than Kyra would like. If she knew something about this place, she wants to know now. But this is the trust that chosen family requires.

"Yeah," Kyra says. "Let's stay in the first theater, though. We spent time enough in there that if something bad were to happen, it would've."

Kyra keeps her blades drawn as she leads the Scroungers back to Theater 4. She shines a light ahead for those without the benefit of Augs, flicking it off when she rediscovers Silver's spent cum soaking the floor. Not the visual she wants before bed.

"Let's keep to the mezzanine," she says, pulling them up the stairs. "Safer."

She hopes no one sees Silver's leavings. They all know what she does, but not everyone wants to know how the pig's skinned.

Less than a minute later, the group is settled against the back wall, packs stashed under their heads.

Kai starts snoring before Kyra can even turn off her lowlight setting.

"I could go down on you," Sprout whispers in her ear, voice full of glee.

"Mmm," she murmurs, pulling them closer. "I wouldn't mind that. What do you want to go down on?"

The dark doesn't stop her from seeing Sprout's pause. It was a question she asked her clients, but it bothered Sprout when she asked it. As a Swapper, one function of her BioAugs allowed her to change the appearance of her genitals. It was a blessing at first, as a woman born with a dick who didn't want one, but it could also be a curse to be fetishized by clients who only wanted her with *that* thing.

"You know I love your body in any shape," Sprout says, annoyance in their tone. "I just want you to be comfortable in it."

It was a level of sweetness Kyra was unused to, a security that contrasted with the chaos of her sex-working Scrounger life. And it was one reason she loved them so much.

"I know, I know," she says, kissing their nose before shimmying out of her baggy cargos. She spreads her legs, then spreads her lips as she pulls Sprout's head down into her already wet pussy.

———

EVEN AFTER CUMMING, Kyra can't sleep. Maybe it's just her alert nature, being in an unknown place like this, but something about this empty theater seems like a façade, an edgeworn sticker spanked over something sinister. She can't help but think about what she saw through the projector window earlier. Or didn't see. The window that lingers temptingly above Sprout's sleeping form. She pushes herself up to her knees and look past the glass, though she's done so innumerable times already. Nothing. She stands up and stretches, strolling down the back aisle to the descending stairs. She hadn't even dimmed her lowlight yet. This feeling is too intense for her to let that much of her guard down.

Awake with nothing else to do, Kyra explores the front of the theater, really looking for the first time at the shredded screen that slouches on the wall like the web of some cybernetic spider. To the touch, it feels like some sort of polyvinyl with a grainy coating. She couldn't tell from a distance, but pin-prick perforations decorate its entirety. The fabric is nothing special, not like the seat coverings, but the method is unusual. As long as Kyra has known, the nanolit polyglass screens that cover nearly every surface of the city have been the norm for vid display. Projection, even for large scales like this, is practically ancient.

Kyra investigates both entryways without finding a projection room access door, but now that the thought has been kindled, she has to see inside. Ancient digital tech like this could sell big to the right buyer. She could snag a piece for proof and find a lead later.

She steps into the main hallway. Even with her lowlight on, the place looks dark. Whatever powered this place has long since fried, leaving a concrete husk devoid of light. Past the next theater, she finally finds a door marked *Employee's Only*. How quaint. She tries it, but the handle shudders grumpily. Locked. Amazing the mechanism hasn't corroded over the years. Luckily, a locked door has never kept Kyra out. She pulls out a pick designed for doors that still use mechanical tumblers. They're rare, but the poor and the paranoid often rely on them instead of the electromag locks that have become the standard.

The tip of the pick clicks along the inner keys as Kyra works it in. She can feel the fragility of the thing. If it wasn't broken before, it will be when she's done with it, deftness be damned. Once she hears the final click, she stands and opens the door. Dark stairs lead into a darker space above. Kyra takes the first step with relish.

The room sucks her in like octopus ink. Devoid of any windows except for the tinted projector glass, this small dark nook inside a large dark nook sucks Kyra in, happy to be filled for the first time in centuries. Even with her lowlight implants activated, she struggles to see. It must be so pitch in here that they're falling short of enough light to augment. The room seems small, half taken up by the towering, human-sized digital projector, but even so the far wall is just out of sight. Cables and wires snake across the cement floor, causing Kyra to trip more than once as she approaches the ancient tech. It looms like a crouched android two times standard size.

"Whoa," she says audibly.

The syllable bounces around the small room and jumps back into her throat.

It's strange to see something like this up close, a dusty husk that was once the peak of technology. She feels how elder generations must have felt when they uncovered the mechanism and mastery of the prehistoric Egyptians. The thing is simultaneously impressive and quaint. Compared to current tech, this giant is a relic, yet despite that she can't help but respect the ingenuity that went into it.

She places a hand on it, feels the solid sheet metal that is a myth nowadays. To the touch, it feels like what a pre-Collapse automobile must have felt like.

Kyra searches for a piece she can easily disconnect. Something identifiable as ancient that wouldn't ruin the projector if it was removed. Someone will pay big to be brought here, she's certain. This could be the payday that changes things for her, for Sprout, for all of them. She opens a panel to reveal what must be the operating controls. A handful of buttons, a switch, a key insert that must've allowed it to only be operated by the keyholder. The key, of course, is missing. She presses a few of the buttons. They hold their place, so unused to movement that it takes a second try to make them budge. She flicks the switch, which, in contrast, gives immediately. It lights up red, and the projector comes to life with a smatter of accelerating clicks. Through the projector window, she can see the screen light up. It's still blank and black, but the difference between that and it being off is noticeable.

"Fuck," Kyra says.

She hopes she didn't wake anyone up. They need sleep.

She presses her face against the glass and looks down. Sprout and the others seem to be snoozing still. Good.

She returns to the control panel and switches the thing off. It doesn't go. She tries more, rapid-fire, but the screen in the theater still glows with life.

She looks at her feet, trying to find the cable that must power this thing. They still had cables in the twentieth, right?

When Kyra finds the decrepit cable, she follows it toward the wall. To her surprise, it concludes with a splayed, wire-infested bloom a few feet before. Must've been chewed by rodents, back when they were still alive.

Huh. As far as she knows, something this size and age should've been powered by a cable. Beyond yanking at a power source, she has no idea how to turn the thing off.

After pacing a moment ineffectivly, Kyra pockets one of the steel button casings and a bit of rogue cable and makes her way out of the projection room. If the light from the blank screen didn't wake the other Scroungers, it shouldn't hurt to have the thing on while they slept. Might even be better, them being as used to the eternal glow of the city as they were.

She reaches the back row and drops herself in the space next to Sprout. She was right. The light of the screen is a comfort compared to the total darkness of before. She closes her eyes finally, letting the subtle buzz of ancient electricity lull her to sleep. In that unknowable moment before she falls, though, something darker than the dimly lit darkness coils over itself like a black snake squirming in the night.

———

KYRA AWAKES when the air becomes thick. She coughs like she'd just hit a harsh vape, the racking of her chest dragging her out of sleep. Instinctually, she blinks on her lowlight view, scanning the theater for any sign of intrusion. It takes a moment for her to realize the two things that are now missing: the light of the silverscreen and Sprout. Kyra isn't able to hold onto her standard calm. She panics in her sleep-stunned state, standing to scan the theater for them with her pulse reader.

A knock behind her interrupts the search. She spins on a razor's edge to face the projector window. With a digital creak, the lens on the other side crackles to life. Kyra spins again to catch the image that overtakes the screen. It's Sprout, short hair blooming from their skull. Their eyes are black, all black, like the gutterpunks who paid for scleral tattoos. Sprout had never had those.

"Down…." the Sprout on screen says, the word crackling out. "Base…."

The words emanate from the dust-encrusted speakers on the wall like they were recorded on an ancient audio interface.

As if in response to her silent question, the entry doors on both sides of the theater begin to glow. Even if it were day, there wouldn't be enough light reaching here to illuminate them that much, and likely it wouldn't look so pink.

Kyra jerks to action. She steps toward the sleeping twins, startled momentarily by the feel of slime below her boots. The fire of her panic catches too quickly for her to consider what she's standing on. She shakes Mai awake, stopping to yell only one word before stomping towards the glowing doors.

"Sprout!"

She hopes the message gets through, but she doesn't stay to find out. She's out the door before hearing anything but a stirring.

Outside, the hallway is illuminated in pale pink. The light glows from the far end of the hall like Kyra is in a cave, and the source is deeper in. She chases after it.

The hall T's at the end, and Kyra nearly slams into the wall as she skids on more of the enigmatic muck. She takes half a moment to look down each hall, long enough to see that the light only glows in the left one. She pushes off the wall and sprints towards its conclusion, pulling free her twin plasma blades from their home on her belt.

The hall is not long, and at the end sits a solid metal door rimmed in neon pink light. Wherever Sprout is, they must be through that door. Still sprinting, Kyra prepares to spring up, jumping and shoving her boots through the air at the door. Her bet pays off. As the thick soles make contact with metal, the dilapidated door frame creaks and gives way, though the impact causes her to fall back to the ground. She lands painfully on one of her blades, the tip of it inserting itself in her side.

"Fuck," she hisses as she pulls it out.

She stands up to hear Dex's voice coming from the main hall. "Kyra?"

"Here!" she yells.

Then she plunges down the neon pink stairway that leads further into the earth.

———

Kyra's boots hit the bottom with the muffled sound of a jaw-punch. Not the clang or concrete smack she'd anticipated the basement of the ruin would make. When she looks down, she sees the blood dripping from her side mix with a thick layer of the sourceless slime. The floor is covered with it, as are the walls, pale but constant with their pink glow.

The light's not brighter down here, but it is more intense. Thicker, somehow, as if contact with the sunless air made it crystallize. Kyra pulls on the fabric mask she wears around her neck by habit. She'll do Sprout no good if she breathes in anything toxic.

"Kyra?"

It's Sprout's voice. It emanates from the only door the walls host, an unhinged hunk hanging off the far wall. They don't sound scared, but they do sound... disoriented, maybe? Which is strange, considering Sprout is the sort that would scream at a spider.

"Kyra!"

The second time makes her take a step. She didn't notice it before, but the walls are webbed with what looks like neon veins, roots maybe, glowing under the surface of the slime. When Sprout speaks, it's as if they brighten with each syllable.

"I'm coming!" Kyra calls, both to Sprout and the group of their friends she hoped was behind her.

She starts to run towards the far wall, her thick-soled boots splashing pink muck everywhere as they land. Through the door, and she stops a moment to get her bearing. There are three doors here, all open.

"Kyra?" Sprout calls quieter now. The voice is misplaced enough that it offers little in direction. She blinks on her pulse finder, but quickly blinks it off as her field of view is taken over by bright yellow-red. She still sees the afterglow for a moment. Her pulse finder shouldn't be malfunctioning. The only thing that would blow it out like that is if she was completely surrounded by signs of life, but as far as she can tell, she's alone.

Except for….

"Where are you?"

Sprouts voice again, punctuated by the pulse-like glow of the slime-webbed walls. Could that be why?

Carefully, she tests the nearest wall with the tip of one of her knives. It gives a slight pop as it bursts the thin skin holding the slime together. Thick juice slides out of the fresh opening. Kyra checks her blade to ensure it isn't corroding before she reaches towards the wall with her open palm. As her skin makes contact, she feels the slight give of a waterbed with a beating underfeel.

Ba-bum. Ba-bum.

As if it's alive. The beat quickens to match her own, and soon the pulse in her palm and that of the walls are indistinguishable.

Kyra? Sprout asks again, but this time their voice echoes inside her skull.

Where are you? She responds, wordlessly.

Follow the brightest vein.

The ceiling snakes with slimy roots, and Kyra now notices the main branch that runs through the middle of the ceiling like a spine. It runs from the door she just entered to the one yawning open to her left, giving birth to tributaries at intervals.

Her heart beats, and the walls beat with it. It calms her, and she sheaths her knives carefully before continuing to follow the main vein, fingertips playfully brushing the walls as she passes.

Somewhere outside of all this she can hear Mai and Dex shouting for her, asking where she is, but their words sink into the gum-thick walls and leave no trace of their existence.

Through the next door, the basement opens up, quite literally. What once was a small storage room has fallen open to marry with some sort of underground cave. Cinderblock bleeds into stone and dark earth, all dressed in a healthy layer of slime. The large space still glows, though less so, as if in its natural habitat the stuff doesn't feel the need to scream for attention. The ceiling is maybe twenty feet high, no more, but the cavern stretches for as far as Kyra can see, concluding in a collection of tunnels leading away in a mixed directions. A hundred yards ahead, lying as if asleep in a viscous puddle, Sprout's form heaves with a weighted breath. Their back is to Kyra, but their form is unmistakable.

Sprout! she calls out telepathically.

Ba-bum ba-bum. The beating of the liquid veins coating every surface is amplified in this open space, making Sprout's lack of response even more drastic.

Kyra leaps toward where they lie, hopping goatlike from rock to rock, avoiding the divots and pools that pock the ground. She reaches them and kneels, her hand finding that their form is cold, sticky, and wet. Movement, even in the smallest scale, is absent from their body. Though Sprout is much bigger than her, Kyra musters the strength to turn them onto their back. A wet, mucky sound punctuates her shock as their lack of face is revealed. The face she loved so much has been eaten away as if by acid, and Sprout's skull lays open like a bowl of red stew left out too long. She draws a knife instinctively, and tries not to think about how hot her face feels.

Kyra can see that whatever ate at them is still having its effect, and as she watches what's left of their brain melts into the air.

Sprout.

She can't help but feel that this is how they would want to go, slowly becoming a part of the earth, soon to be free from the cityscape they so despised. But she can't let them go. Not yet.

She knows it's useless, but she puts an ear to their scarred chest, listening for a beat beyond the one emanating from the walls.

Kyra!

The direction of the telepathic speech is incongruent with her location. It almost seems like it has come from one of the tunnels that branches out from the cavern. Before she can respond, the cave begins to shake, vibrating with the movement of something massive.

Kyra stands, biting her cheek to combat the pain caused by the wound in her side. She slides her second blade out of her belt and grips each handle tightly.

Whatever's coming, she wants a piece of it.

As the earth shimmies harder, the farther tunnel begins to emanate a low hum, an enigmatic sound that could be a creature's call or the mechanics of movement screaming for survival. Her answer comes when the empty black entrance to the tunnel is replaced by an equally round, equally empty orifice. A large, intestinal opening that couldn't belong to anything vertebrate.

Before she can leap to attack, Sprout's body stirs at her feet. She was certain they were dead. Couldn't be alive with a wound like that.

Sprout pushes themself up and regards Kyra with an absent face before turning to walk towards the oncoming creature.

"What the fuck are you doing?" she screams, aloud this time.

She rushes towards them and knocks them aside. The body stutters its steps before resuming its course towards the gaping mouth. As if it is salivating, the creature begins to drip pink slime. Muck oozes from its opening as well as the pale skin that's becoming visible as it slides itself out of the hole. As more of its body is revealed, Kyra can see it in detail. To call it a worm would communicate the surface of its premise, but hardly the totality. It's tubular, like a worm, and it writhes toward Kyra and Sprout like a worm of that size would, but its skin isn't smooth like she'd expect. It looks like white sandpaper, and as it exits the tunnel, she sees that this is how this cave was made. It's gritty surface slides against the earth, turning anything solid to dust as it does. Pink slime coats the ground-down edges of the tunnel, and the thing expands as it frees itself from the smaller space, growing to fill more than half of the cave before her. What was once a double-wide door of a mouth becomes the size of a traffic tunnel.

Kyra grips the puny blades in her hands, unable to move as what used to be Sprout shambles as if summoned into the gut-churning maw. By their second step into it, the creature closes, contracting the edges of its mouth to consume the person she loves.

She drops her blades and falls to her knees. It's only too clear what will happen here. The pale behemoth is now yards away, its mouth dilating to reveal the melting skeleton of her lover as it slips deeper into the beast, carried by undulations that shudder the walls.

Kyra's not one to fight losing battles, so she doesn't. Instead, she chooses to close her eyes, remembering one of the first times she and Sprout kissed. It was on top of the tallest building on the short side of downtown, a residential/commercial hybrid from which they had pilfered dinner together. They'd ran to the roof to escape the security drones, guessing correctly that their algorithms would lead them towards the building's entrance once the perpetrators were out of view. Despite their careful nature, Sprout had taken the chance, asking her if they could kiss her as the weather-screen overhead began its allotted drizzle of spring-time rain. She didn't always like getting wet, but she suffered it for the feel of their lips on hers. So different than what she'd done for money. The real thing to the facsimile that was every john she'd taken. Afterwards, they'd grasped hands as they jumped the six feet down to the next building's roof and began their descent back into the dirty belowparts of the city, alone within it for the last time.

She's already decided she can't leave them alone here, either, drastic as the circumstances are. She stands to greet demise like Sprout had. Willingly and with plodding steps. The way her soles melt as she steps into the yawning mouth warms her feet in a way that's almost comforting. An alien sensation averse to the cold digits the Cascadian cityscape often left you with. She wishes she could hold Sprout again, all of them, but she has to settle for laying down next to their acid-burnt bones and spooning them. The buzz she feels is both the ecstasy of closeness and the pain of being digested by the creature's juices. The last thing she sees before her eyeballs pop is what teeth Sprout's skull still houses.

Her last thought is how much she loves their smile.

———

THE CONSUMPTION OF MAI, Kai, and Dex is like watching a vid in a dark room. An isolated, moving image of them running into the cavern a minute after Sprout and Kyra are gone. Imagine this perspective as a fly on the wall. A vein in the slime. The Digester's mouth yawns before them, and they charge in maybe without even realizing the cave had ended and their end had begun. As the edges close around them, so do the edges of the image, blacking out like the final shot of a scene.

But you are part of it. You know, know so well, that the film is far from over.

A MARRIAGE OF BLOOD AND PUS

CHARLES AUSTIN MUIR

YOU WORK with what you've got; Nielsen Nasino worked with his wife's massage office.

The middle-aged couple could have used a space in their house for his ministrations. The "hoarder's nest," probably, his grandmother's study long before he inherited the family home. That painted a heinous picture... Nielsen changing bandages amidst disused furniture and worn-out shoes, while their aging Chihuahuas sniffed under the French doors and soiled the living-room carpet. The last thing the Nasinos needed was more scatological disorder; they spent enough time managing excreta.

Fortunately, they had the massage office beneath the rental unit they'd built at the rear of the property, before Rae learned she had cancer. Mornings and evenings, since the abscesses started, Nielsen would leave his house by the side door, punch in the security code and enter the spa his wife had made for a vanished clientele—a sanctuary of incense and crystals that suggested healing, but raised questions of a lost future. Rae would wait patiently for him, lying face down on her massage table wearing an open-shoulder top and a bath towel. Her glistening ivory skin made him think of a client who expected a service other than massage, or at least one in addition to it... certainly not the one he intended to perform.

As though it were a horror movie, they called his task "the stuffening."

At first it *had* seemed like a horror movie, their neighbor—a wound care nurse, by a stroke of luck—showing Nielsen how to stuff a gauze strip into the surgical incision in Rae's left buttock to draw pus from the abscess. On his first attempt, his wife gasped and bright red spurted onto her inner thigh, a gruesome visual in the style of Italian film director Dario Argento.

But after that traumatic start, they settled into Rae's wound care with such efficiency that Nielsen would breeze in and arrange his instruments between her legs with barely a word.

One night, catching her on the phone, he set to work behind her in utter silence, like a psychopathic surgeon in a giallo film. Which amused him afterward, yet disturbed him as a sign his hands were growing alien to him. How would he ever have sex with Rae again if he became the boogeyman in endless, pus-soaked sequels of *The Stuffening*?

Endless: The word took much for granted.

———

METASTATIC CANCER WAS LIKE A DESERT, its treatment like a military invasion guided by conflicting maps and incomplete simulations. As a caregiver, Nielsen worked in the fractures of those simulations, the dead ends left by those bulging aftercare folders the surgeons handed out, fictions that described a static terrain without irregularities or contingencies. He grew so comfortable in the interstices that tending to his wife's wounds felt more real to him than anything else; at times he felt inspired, as if he could lead them to remission through his competence with suture scissors. Yet he knew this—his makeshift medical station, his ever-evolving method—was a simulation in itself, an illusion of personal control.

Even that illusion wavered when the next crisis struck: A trip to the Emergency Room culminating in Rae's ninth time under the knife since she began treatment. A special team used guided imaging to place a catheter in a major abscess discovered near

her uterus. Thankfully, the drainage unit required few adjust-
ments on the home-nursing front. But it raised questions about
her patient status: How long could the oncology team postpone
chemotherapy to aid recovery from its "minimally invasive"
mutilations? And even if chemo continued, how many more
times would the surgeons slice Rae open before they decided
enough was enough?

Her tortured pelvis wasn't a franchise Nielsen could star in
indefinitely—yet what could he could do but play *The Stuffener*
unless fresh hands were brought in for a revamp?

As the weeks wore on, Nielsen performed his duties in a
trance-like state, like a moviegoer pantomiming actions in a film
playing over and over. Squirt, snip, pack, spritz, tape, repeat, the
glint of steel in blue-gloved hands evoking a murder mystery
abbreviated like the narrative elisions of a '90s porn compilation
video. Sealed off from the outside world, the massage office
became an exteriorization of the theater in Nielsen's inner eye, a
retreat into a type of cinema that referred to nothing outside its
parodic gestures of anonymous violence. This gave him a
narcotic escape maintaining the *absence* of emotional experience.

To ritualize his role otherwise would have thrown him into
unbearable episodes of anxiety and depression.

———

BEYOND THE MASSAGE OFFICE, *the desert spread in all directions…*

———

SUSPENDED in the loop between viewer and subject, spectator
and puppet-actor, Nielsen watched Rae's wounds improve with
growing disinterest. Her body became a souvenir of the "film"
that kept him sane, a plastic reference to an abstract, pseudo-
violent spectacle. Merging his experience with an artistic experiment arrested his terrors of a time-bound universe. Outside the
loop, past and future lay like mirror images of a ruins too vast
and horrifying to confront, a blighted landscape of necrotic

processes and surgical alterations as if neither side could escape Rae's malignant disease.

To look at his wife as someone with a history made him picture a gravestone; worse, to see her empathetically brought waking nightmares of human vivisection, a series of rationalized atrocities leading toward the end of mutual desire, not only for sex but for any experience beyond the house, the massage office, and ultimately the hospice.

As Rae's outer wounds healed, Nielsen's inner ones festered. He exchanged few words with his wife, drank late into the night and treated every task as an imitation of *The Stuffening* loop. Cleaning up dog turds, loading the dishwasher, answering emails… sequences recycled from a forgotten purpose, a self-referential play of forms. Like the animated graphic he'd seen of the primary tumor once, a bright, dense pattern that made him sob, to his surprise; after all, it couldn't possibly refer to a life-threatening substance inside his wife's rectum—an alien invader in an old video game, perhaps.

Not cancer.

The effects of so many surgeries—or more precisely, the limitations they forced him to consider—shook his hopes for a better life so deeply that his only solace came from scrambling the logic of his actions into a cipher known only to the free-floating, inscrutable *Stuffener*. Parodies of his post-surgical paro-dying, his motions became exercises of pure gesture with nothing to be gained or lost… nothing to be felt, only looped, like the mock boogeyman he could never fully become.

But as he had learned in art school—and again, looking at the digital blob in a radiologist's office—sooner or later, the medita-tive response to a novel pattern cracks open and emotion breaks through.

And finally, late one morning, it happened. Nielsen had finished cleaning up and started heading toward the door when Rae seized his hand. He looked down at the figure on the table as if a driftwood sculpture—like the cavernous monstrosity he'd bought at a county fair two summers ago—had grabbed hold of him. For the first time in weeks, he saw the light of a living being before him. The tousled hair, freckled cheeks, hazel eyes, ignited a flame of recognition that burned through his celluloid dream and engulfed him in a blazing deathtrap of his own making.

"What's wrong," he said.

"Me," she said. "I'm disgusting."

———

THAT NIGHT, while Rae slept on the couch, Nielsen got stinking drunk.

He couldn't stop seeing the look she had given him. The tremor in her jaw, tears welling in her eyes. In a flash he saw he had failed her again: Objectified her, treated her like a discarded prop, a fixed, inanimate quantity outside his imaginary film loop, incapable of feeling, insensate except perhaps in some reflexive way, like a sea anemone under stress; at its realest, nothing more than an ecosystem of infections and medical scarifications.

"You must think I'm a monster," she had told him, after his last infidelity five years ago. When her words had finally made him realize his power to summon childhood ghosts… hers *and* his.

Rae was of Scandinavian descent and stood nearly six feet. By contrast, Nielsen's feminine ideal revolved around petite, doe-eyed brown women, an antithesis that made his wife feel like "the Blob" again, the cruel nickname she'd received after her first growth spurt in middle school. They both recognized— much as he hated to admit it—that his deceitfulness stemmed from a need to recover the past as it stared sullenly from the faded Polaroids he kept in a shoebox under the bed. But knowing Nielsen eroticized his lost mother did nothing to mitigate Rae's shame when she caught her husband carrying on illicit correspondences with women who looked like Barbara Perez—an actress known as "the Audrey Hepburn of the Philippines."

Nielsen yearned for a restless princess, like the Perez lookalike (Vanessa Templonuevo—a name that meant nothing and yet everything) in his hand-me-down photographs, unwilling to welcome the piece of the future growing inside her.

"Why do you stay with me," Rae said, after she had caught him in a year-long texting relationship with an ex-co-worker. "I don't look anything like these dream girls you like to chase. I'm hideous and in the way... like the troll in the fairy tale." A Norwegian fairy tale, no less: Rae's ancestry.

A monster.

I'm the monster, Nielsen thought, working on his seventh glass of wine while a grainy Filipino horror movie played on the television. Catching only a smattering of the dubbed Tagalog, he watched a snaggled-toothed old man dancing with a Filipina Audrey Hepburn at a barbecue about to be overrun by machete-wielding zombie bikers (a campy Americanism in a gratuitous subplot). That was himself on the screen, he thought; the grizzled lecher patting the young lady's bottom and croaking evil propositions before the zombie gang's leader stabbed him in the back. *Justice*. But it was all downhill from there. The girl, simultaneously gored by the blow, backing away screaming... the old man crawling toward a picnic table, bubbling inanities... the ravenous, leather-clad outlaws turning the idyllic scene into a bloodbath. All captured with shaky camera work that made Nielsen feel dizzy. Not only that, his rising anger made him feel hot.

Still asleep, Rae shook the blanket off her and sighed.

Nielsen watched her, then left his rocking chair to get another glass of wine. When he sat in front of the TV again, the yard was littered with corpses and the undead bikers were slaughtering live goats. *What's with Filipino filmmakers and animal cruelty*, he thought. The shaky camera zoomed in to show one of the animals twitching as a rusty blade pierced its heart. *Garbage*. Not just the unnecessary act, but its voyeuristic presentation made Nielsen want to jump through the television screen and cut the filmmakers' throats. But he let the shitty movie play, not taking his eyes from it as he pulled out the butterfly knife he had brought back from the kitchen.

Sweat pouring down his neck, he flipped the knife open and pointed it at the real animal murderers in bad zombie makeup and ill-fitting biker attire. Narrowing his eyes to slits, he visualized slipping through a portal into the film and sticking the blade between the skinny Filipino actors' ribs, puncturing their livers.

I'm the motherfucking monster, Nielsen thought, aiming his vengeful desire at the gory spectacle on the television.

He flipped the knife point-down and grinned.

————

THE NEXT DAY, Nielsen woke with a nasty hangover and a painful itch in his left fingers. Squeamishly, he held his hand up as if inspecting a manicure and waited for his eyes to adjust to the bedroom light. He saw what he expected: Several knuckle cuts from playing a game he'd watched his father play with friends after his mother had run off. Years later, he would learn it had names like "five finger fillet" and a history of mortally wounding players before antibiotics were discovered, but his father simply called it "reflex practice" and played it with an air of impatience, even boredom.

Nielsen remembered the four men, fish cannery workers as weathered as the houses they rented, vying for dominance at the cedar table his great-grandfather had built as a wedding gift for his parents. His father always came out on top, reaching speeds incomprehensible to the three-year-old boy spectating breathlessly through the beaded curtain hanging in the doorway. In retrospect, it was an incredibly stupid contest, considering the group played music as a side hustle. Equipped with a sharp object, the player laid his palm flat on a tabletop, spread his fingers and stabbed the spaces between them. Working from thumb to little finger, each player repeated the sequence at higher speeds until he felt he had maxed out or hurt himself. His father's group—a jazz quartet that enjoyed playing complex patterns—took the game a step further: They repeated the stab behind the thumb after every stab between fingers and finished each sequence by working back in reverse order, rather than skipping back to the beginning.

It made for hair-raising contests.

A cigarette dangling from his mouth and a can of cheap beer in his lap, his father would thread the needle of bone and connective tissue as if in a trance; perhaps that was his secret to success, Nielsen thought, flexing his fingers and breaking the scabs open. Aggrieved by his wife's desertion, escaping into a cinematic fantasy of self-mutilation, suspended in a loop between viewer and puppet-actor... unconcerned for his well-being, his father had played the game close to perfection. Unlike Nielsen last night, so drunk he could barely keep his eyes open, adrenaline coursing through his veins, enraged by that stupid movie, the old man and the zombie bikers slaughtering live goats... he'd ended up spitting a wine-laced loogie and flinging his blood at the television screen. Then he'd snuck off to bed and bloodied the beige sheets while Rae dozed on the couch, undisturbed by his grotesque imitation of his father, for he had placed his left hand on a leatherbound Bible (bloodying the cover painting of the Last Supper considerably), a family heirloom, to muffle the knife sounds.

I can't afford to mess up like this, he thought, watching blood trickle down the back of his hand.

Who knew how badly his father might have injured himself playing "reflex practice" if he had lived long enough?

She needs me. She can't have The Stuffener turning on himself. Dumb.

Or was it? For the first time in weeks, he had *felt* something: Unadulterated rage. Pure Filipino vengefulness brewed in the blood of a warrior culture. Passion that sharp and deep rises above fear... and he had lived in fear for so long. Terrified of what lay beyond the desert of cancer, he had fled into a form of self-induced mesmerism like his heartbroken father. To be sure, it made life bearable seeing Rae's wounds as elements within an empty cinematic violence, rather than as clues to an affliction with her life at stake. Yet wounds were a driving force of the

Filipino spirit; to deny that was to be wounded yet again. If he hurt himself, he harmed Rae, too.

This far into the desert, she needed everything Nielsen could give her. Not just his mechanical competence, but his willingness to participate, to return to *desire*. Even if that steered him back to his mother's legacy of heartbreak… to another shoebox under the bed.

Nielsen rolled over into a sitting position and wiped his bloody hand on his thigh. The red smears on his brown skin made him smile. *So fucking beautiful*, he thought. All this time, the remedy to his psychic sickness had literally been right under his nose. *Desire*. In the form of vengefulness, it had led him to the gashes on his hands; those wounds could lead him back to the desire he and Rae needed to carry on.

A vision was forming in his mind, a marriage of blood and pus, a love story for the ages. Not exactly what he pictured when he vowed to love and honor Rae all the days of his life, but whatever.

You work with what you've got.

————

"I TOLD you my dad got into the occult, right?" Nielsen asked, stuffing his wife's left gluteal incision.

"I don't remember," Rae said.

"Yeah, he bought a bunch of books on spell-casting after my mom left him. They're in the hoarder's nest. I thought I told you about this."

"You might have. How does it smell back there?"

Nielsen sniffed at the stale air; he detected only the chlorine scent of wound cleanser and a faint odor from the medical waste bag on the floor.

"Not bad," he said.

"Good."

"Anyway, I'm thinking I might go through them to see if there's anything I can use for a project."

"An art project?"

"Yeah… hold on."

This was the tricky part of the routine. Frowning in concentration, he picked up his suture scissors, angled the bottom blade above the cauliflower-like wound bed verging on the gluteal cleft, and with a sharp intake of breath, snipped off the gauze.

"Boom," he said.

"Nielsen," she said.

"Hmm?

"I love you."

"Love you, too."

He tossed the leftover gauze and cotton swab into the trash bag and picked up another swab and roll of tape from the underpad between Rae's thighs. As he repeated the process with the opposite incision, he thought how much easier this had been when he'd worked in a trance, like his father playing "reflex practice" with a razor-sharp Pakal knife.

Another snip millimeters from the wound opening; done.

"That makes me happy you want to do something creative again," Rae said, as he dumped his paraphernalia back into the box. "Your life can't be all about my cancer. Do you think you might want to go back to teaching?"

"I can't see how, with everything we're dealing with," Nielsen said, rummaging through the box for a one-piece wound dressing. "Shit. I think we ran out of EZ Guard."

"That's okay. Home Health will send us more tomorrow."

"Well, you're *stuffened*, anyway."

"Thank you."

He draped Rae's buttocks again with her bath towel.

"Oh—and I should tell you I cut myself playing with the knife last night," he said.

"Bad?"

"Well, not good."

"Do we need to take you to the ER?"

"Oh, God."

They had been to the emergency room three times in the last month; the thought of going back for Nielsen made them break out laughing.

"No, but it would make life easier if you helped me replace all my Band-Aids," he said.

"You've got to be more careful with that thing," Rae said.

"My fingers itch like hell."

"After you wash your hands, you should rub in some of that petroleum jelly you use on my ass crack."

Nielsen started rooting through the box again, thought about her advice and chuckled.

"I know," Rae said. "We're quite a pair. Go find a spell in one of your dad's books that'll make it so you can get away from me for a while."

"That is not what I had in mind for my art project."

―――――

ALONE IN THE DEN, sadly aware his Chihuahuas were soiling the living-room carpet again, Nielsen moved his grandmother's armchair away from the window and opened the corner closet. Tucked in the back, behind storage bins, bags of comic books and cassette tapes, and a 1950s console television, he found the cardboard box containing his college textbooks and teaching materials as well as what remained of the ancestral library. He dragged the hulking box into the room's center and sorted through its contents.

An hour later, he had pulled out seventy years' worth of reading, including hardcover editions of *Tom Sawyer* and *A Streetcar Named Desire* translated into Tagalog, and several issues of *Ginoo*, "the Filipino Man's Magazine." All that remained were pulp paperbacks, a folding map of the Philippines, three occult books (why had he expected to find five times as many?), and a small notebook: His father's. It had never drawn his eye for some reason; he had peeked into it maybe once while reorganizing the closet years ago. Now, he stared at the black leather cover as if it contained the key to his "art project."

In the living room, the dogs barked halfheartedly at the coupons and catalogs inching through the mail slot.

Nielsen closed his fingers on the rubber band around the

miniature binder. The brittle rubber broke at his touch. Flipping through the opening pages, he found lists of venues, hotels, and phone numbers in his father's spidery hand, interspersed with blue ink scribbles so violent the pen tip had torn through the paper. A gap of blank pages intervened, then the lists resumed in red marker. Costs, set lists, music shops, packing lists covering everything from cigarettes to music gear. After his mother had run off, his father had tried to become a full-time musician rather than go on getting fired from back-breaking labor jobs. Nielsen remembered him coming home from touring and drinking so hard he'd black out in the front yard.

More blank pages.

The next section was filled with words copied alphabetically from a dictionary. Another gap followed, broken by touring lists obscured by a coffee spill that had bled through several sheets. As Nielsen leafed through them, making out a word here and there ("spare chords," [sic] "Stratocaster,") he noticed a space between the final pages. He wedged his bandaged middle finger into it and spread the pages open. A sheet of folded typing paper lay between them. He was certain he had never examined it before.

He unfolded the sheet. In the upper right-hand corner was a date and time: *June 11, 6:00.* No mention of a year or which side of noon the hour had fallen on. In the left margin, two spaces down, was a greeting: *"Dear Sophia…"* Nielsen lingered over the words, chuckling. When it came to romancing women from afar, he was a chip off the old block. He might have even learned from his old man: Scanning the contents, he found words from the dictionary lists and a flowing cursive that contradicted his memory of Nestor Nasino's rough-hewn speech and mannerisms. Tickled by his father's poetical prowess, Nielsen skimmed the letter for a general impression, then reread it slowly to digest a meaning or tie a reference to a childhood memory.

He learned a great deal about the correspondents' relationship. They had met when his father was on tour. The woman had enchanted him: Nestor had never seen such an example of "pulchritude" (a dictionary word) as Sophia when a mutual friend introduced them. In addition to being pulchritudinous, the enchantress was a superb opera singer. Indeed, if fate were to rob him of sight, his father declares, he would soar on the pleasures of her voice in a heaven of darkness.

His father goes on to tell Sophia about his emotional state after Vanessa, his wife, deserted him six years earlier.

This happened a week after she gave birth to their son. The shock was so profound that he withdrew into a trance-like state, a numbness that made him lazy and hard-hearted. During this period, he let his mother do the child-rearing (*true*, Nielsen thought), took to drinking heavily (*like a middle-aged frat boy*), and treated his fellow man like puppets in a malicious play, a mean-spirited parody of the follies of love (*oh, come on, Dad*). His actions pointed toward an early grave... but then Providence sent him Sophia, his "Byronesque peach" (*ugh*); like an angel, she revived him with her sweet words and celestial song (*to say nothing of her pulchritude*). The only problem he still faced was "the sensual energy lying dormant within him," which his wife had nearly extinguished.

Never fear, though—Nestor vows he will stop at nothing to get the current flowing again:

Have you heard of sigils, Sophia? I am guessing not. I only learned about them from a book someone left behind after one of the shows. It's called The Ascension of Lust, *by Edward Charles Something-Or-Other. I will send it to you; the artwork is elegant. Anyway, a sigil is a symbol that speaks to your subconscious. The reason you would create one is to produce a change in the universe that reflects a desired outcome. In my case, desire itself is the outcome. Not mere carnal arousal, which is episodic and summoned easily enough, but the flow of mysterious bioelectricity that mirrors the rhythms of nature. I am talking about a connection with the world, a capacity to receive... as I have received you into my life.*

When we meet again, Sophia, I will come to you as a complete man: Awake, vibrant, pulsating.

Nielsen closed his eyes and took a deep breath. *Never again,* he told himself, *use the word 'pulsating.'"

He continued reading:

How will the sigil help me transform? Simple. If I tell myself, "I want to revitalize my sensual energy," I will get tangled up in thoughts about how to make it happen. I will ponder the question to death and worry about it constantly. I will ask myself over and over, "Am I doing it now? Did it happen already? Am I missing something?" On the other hand, if I direct this order to my subconscious, it will work on the problem in the background, without thoughts getting in the way, without worry of what others will think. This is because the subconscious operates outside the order of rationality, morality, and identity.

Free from all that structure, it gathers so much more information than our conscious minds can hold. But you can't boss it around like a sulking teenager. You must speak to it indirectly and symbolically, which is how your subconscious speaks to you when you dream (I dream of you all the time, by the way). This is where the sigil comes in handy. But I don't want to bore you with technical details. All you need to know is I wrote down a statement of intention and converted it into an abstract symbol to bypass my conscious mind. Then I put myself into a trance-like state to "activate" the sigil, or charge it with emotional energy, which is how the intention penetrates the subconscious.

When you're a musician, a trance-like state is easy to achieve. All you have to do is start playing your instrument. After that, focusing on the intention represented by the sigil should activate it. But why stop there? Think how much more energy you can harness when you whip up a crowd of drunks swaying to the noises coming from your guitar! You've got an intention-setting amplifier right under your nose! Well, that was what I thought the other night when I looked at the audience and remembered I kept my sigil in my pocket. A perfect resource for my activation ritual. I waited for my solo to come in. Right before the bridge, I pulled out my scrap of paper and dropped it into the crowd. In the reddish light, the people looked like flames engulfing it. So that is what I imagined: My sigil catching fire in the heat of youthful, sweaty hedonism. The collective excitation in the room charged my little symbol and unleashed its intention on the universe. Not even my bandmates had any clue, and they helped to charge it!

I felt slightly deceitful, but for a good cause. After all, this is the very opposite of the trance I had induced in myself before: Rather than

*retreating from the world, I am running toward it. But I'm not
finished, Sophia. I have created another sigil to build upon the first one.
It involves the Visayan deity* Nagmalitong Yawa Sinagmaling
Diwata, *goddess of lust and seduction. According to some myths about
her, she feeds on the flesh of wandering men; what I know for my sigil
is that she demands the energy of a great many people, not necessarily
living ones...*

———

NIELSEN FOLDED the paper and replaced it in the notebook. He
couldn't believe his father would say nothing more about the
second sigil or the goddess with the long name. Then again,
maybe he should have expected his old man to break off and
praise Sophia's pulchritude again when the letter was getting
interesting... how much of Nielsen's own epistolary mischief
had suffered from rhapsody over substance?

Not that the sentiments would have bothered Sophia, surely,
if the letter had reached her. Why had his father denied her his
carefully constructed declaration of love? Had he sent her a
revised version? And what about *The Ascension of Lust* by Mr.
Something-Or-Other? Had it landed on Sophia's doorstep with
or without some version of the draft his father had tucked away
in his little notebook?

Nielsen rechecked the occult material he'd pulled from the
stacks of Tarzan novels at the bottom of the box. No such title.

Except for the notebook and occult books, he started
returning everything to the box. Despite his frustration, he had
to admit he'd made quite a haul in the last hour: Instead of ideas
for his "art project," he had unearthed a partial grimoire in the
guise of a love letter composed by his father. Not only that, the
emerging father-son parallels gave him hope for his secret
enterprise. Both were love poets at heart. Both searched for a
lost or threatened future. Both used self-hypnosis to escape reality. Both took an interest in ritual magic (Nielsen had played
around with sigils for a college art project). Both found opportunity hiding in plain sight. The linkages formed a chain that

could lead Nielsen back to Rae in a way his father had been denied.

If only Nestor Nasino had steered clear of the Southern Oregon town where cops could shoot a man dead for the crime of being Filipino. Over the years, Nielsen had thought of so many questions to ask him. Judging by his birth reference, his father took a bullet shortly after he had written the letter to Sophia. He might have at least postponed his fateful encounter until after he'd written to her about the second sigil ritual and kept a copy of the update…

As Nielsen stacked the *Ginoo* issues inside the box, he thought of another question: What had his father meant when he wrote, "*She demands the energy of a great many people, not necessarily living ones?*"

Who was this tempting, man-eating goddess?

He made a mental note to look her up online later. He finished packing up the books and returned the box to the closet. Sweating from exertion and excitement, he looked around the room and frowned at the dust motes drifting in front of the window.

"Rae?" He called out. He didn't think she'd come in, but he might not have heard her over his rummaging. "Rae…?"

It figured. He'd had plenty of time to search through the Nasino archive without having to explain himself. He hadn't needed to lie about an art project.

Still, he had enjoyed setting off on his family treasure hunt in secret. It had given him the most fun he'd had in weeks—a sign that he was tapping into his primal nature, coming alive in the depths of despair. By the same token though, he needed to proceed with caution. If he kept more secrets from Rae, he might wake the part of himself that messaged Barbara Perez lookalikes on secret dating apps. Unlike his father, he had lived long enough to learn the power of hidden motivations.

At least this time, he told himself—hearing Rae enter the house, now—he was planning to cheat on his wife *with* her, albeit in a shadowy, unfathomable sense she must never know about.

She would be appalled, perhaps humiliated, to learn what he was plotting. Not that he had any idea what he was plotting, except that it involved a sigil ritual. How and where to conduct it eluded him. He could do it in the house, with Rae in the next room and the dogs barking at the letter carrier… or in the massage office hoping she didn't walk in on him… or in a public place designed for a specific purpose. Going out seemed to be the best option. Then he could avoid personal distractions and harness the power of collective emotions. And if he understood his father's cryptic statement about the goddess, he might be able to charge the sigil with residual energy from *past* events; no need to work with a live crowd.

Weird shit. But, if drawing goofy wizard symbols in public could restore Nielsen to what his father called "dormant sensual energy," so be it.

You work with what you've got.

Idly, he picked up the top book in the occult stack, *Confessions of a Sorceress*, by Honey Slutter. Forget the pseudonym, the cover image of a serpent woman joyously swallowing her tail should have told him the pocketbook belonged in a different pile. The second book was a 1960s paperback reissue of Aleister Crowley's *The Book of Lies*. The third book… he'd recognized it earlier, but hadn't seen its value until he discovered his father's letter. Now, it seemed as if Nestor Nasino were speaking to him across the decades, leading him deeper into the mystery of self-transformation. Heart thudding in his chest, Nielsen ran his itchy fingers over the library-bound tome that had given him nightmares as a child: *Haunted Localities—A Guidebook for the Adventurous Investigator*, by Dr. J. Farnan.

A few minutes later, Rae opened the French doors and glanced from the hefty volume in his hands to the little notebook at his feet.

"What have you got there," she asked.

"I'm going out tonight," he said. "I've got an idea for my art project."

———

AT TEN MINUTES PAST MIDNIGHT, his wife's wounds stuffed and his backpack loaded for his sigil ritual, Nielsen climbed into his van and drove down to the main road. The fact that he was going into town at that hour without Rae made him feel both powerful and foolish. Other than for hospital appointments, he rarely ventured beyond the strip malls and retirement centers encircling the Victorian aerie that three Nasino generations had called home. Now, here he was, cruising at 50 mph, Notorious B.I.G. on the stereo, dressed in baggy jeans and a dark hoodie as if he thought he were a caricature of a young Black gangster and not a middle-aged Asian scared of breaking into an abandoned building.

He almost wished he hadn't found Dr. Farnan's encyclopedia of "haunted localities."

The familiar black-and-white photos of abandoned jails, hospitals, and the like had inspired him to skim through his father's lists again. At the beginning of the notebook, he saw the perfect destination for charging his sigil: *The Picante*. The name revived childhood memories of riding past the then-notorious theater with his father. At the time, the brown brick building bore a yellow sign above the entrance with the Spanish word for "spicy" in red chop suey lettering and a disclaimer that the cinematic marvels within were for *mature adults only*—a promotional enticement not easily understood in the digital age. Fortunately, Nielsen was just old enough to grasp its historical significance: In the 1970s, long before the World Wide Web, filmed scenarios of a "mature" nature weren't instantaneous distractions, but 35-mm group catharses often enhanced by live entertainment… the latter which he learned from a sociology professor years after the decline of the adult movie house.

What a time for porno!

Staring at the venue listing, Nielsen could only assume his father's band must have provided musical background for such canonical triumphs as *Pork Sword* and *Riders of the Purple Sausage*. Imagine a packed auditorium caught in the awkward synchrony between live performance and mechanical interpretation as actors remote in time and place grappled in hypnotic cycles of tension and release on a towering screen… to watch a skin flick in those days must have been quite a diversion. Home video killed adult cinema before Nielsen could observe it (in a dive called the Tapatio, coincidentally) as anything more than an archipelago of Beckettesque loners in a sea of red folding seats, and the Picante became an arcade before the building went up for lease again in the early 2000s; but whatever the clientele, that brief notation in his father's script represented decades of desire being shared and spent in an enclosed space. Surely, someone with a plan and a bag of tricks could exploit the currents that must still linger inside the abandoned building.

But did that someone, who'd never gotten so much as a speeding ticket, have the guts to force entry into the site? Would Nielsen rise to the occasion, so to speak, if the job required him to get his hands dirty?

He was at least desperate enough to hope the Picante's naughty history might supercharge his sigil. Not that the building looked anything but demolition-ready as it became visible in his windshield. He turned down the stereo, "Ready to Die" fading under the noise of the engine and tires chewing gravel as he pulled over in front of a Lebanese market kitty-corner from the ruined landmark. He shut off the engine and stared out the windshield, his heart hammering against his ribs like a cement fist. As the silence dragged on, his instinct kicked in and he took note of his surroundings.

The area had succumbed to gentrification, that was obvious from the increased restaurants and organic grocery stores a few blocks over. High-rent development meant more private security and law enforcement, not necessarily good news for citizens of color (certainly not if they were caught with a butterfly knife and an enormous pry bar). Nevertheless, from what Nielsen saw on his drive into the neighborhood, pockets of the old community clung to life, like the portion of street around him. Booze, bongs, punk records, and body piercings could all be sought here, along with Lebanese wares hidden behind security cameras and iron bars.

True, such protection—as well as the potholes, shattered

glass, and graffiti in the immediate vicinity—suggested conditions ripe for aggressive policing, but from the looks of the former theater he could walk up to its front doors and draw his sigil six feet high in spray paint without anyone interfering. Who cared about a condemned pile of crumbling bricks in those environs? It wasn't like he planned to burgle a cell phone store inside a swanky apartment complex, or the canned halal meat section of a Lebanese grocer, for that matter; he wanted to sneak into an old porn house, do some hocus-pocus and scurry into the night like a rat into a storm drain. Quick and simple.

The street was dead. *Go for it.*

And he was about to round up his equipment when a police siren wailed a few blocks away. Sweating, Nielsen waited for it to die down, watched his side-view as a group of smokers went back into the tavern two blocks behind him and straightened to take in the view through his windshield again: Residential zoning, starting at the next property after the theater. Of course, it figured the neighboring bungalow would be the only house within a thousand feet with its porchlight on, piercing an overgrown hedge, but...

Wait. Something between the shrubs and the building. A car?

He leaned toward the dashboard and strained his eyes to make out the metallic glint in the streetlight. Sure enough, it was the rear bumper of a vehicle parked around the corner from the front entrance. The neighbor's fixer-upper, perhaps, or the building owner's attempt to block a passageway. Of course— there had to be an emergency exit in case of fire. That was his entry point, then. With luck, he could squeeze past the car, pry the fire exit door open and perform the ritual in less time than it took to stuff Rae's wounds.

Throwing on his backpack, he hurried around to the back of the van, opened the doors and picked up his pry bar.

He trained his eyes on the car bumper and marched across the street. The monstrous leg of steel at his side made him feel like a serial killer on the prowl. When he reached the Buick, rather than squeeze past it he climbed onto the trunk and walked over it. Then he jumped down onto the cracked, mossy pavement between the hedge and building and made sure no one watched him from the street.

The path was clear to the concrete wall terminating the passageway. He turned the corner and found the fire exit door. No padlocks, no motion sensor lights, not even a "No Trespassing" sign to deter intruders. With a single wrench on the pry bar, he made the door flex enough for the latch to clear the door strike. His first B & E, and no one witnessed it except for a skunk waddling from behind a rusted steel drum at the passageway's end.

Nielsen shivered.

————

LEAVING THE DOOR AJAR, he crept into the theater with the pry bar in one hand and a lantern in the other. He braced himself for dead bodies, rats, spiders and insects (he even fancied he saw a snake for an instant), but after his nerves settled, he realized the auditorium looked in decent shape. Other than a cobwebbed ceiling and a floor littered with fallen plaster, he couldn't find a thing that reminded him of Dr. Farnan's spooky localities. As if the previous vendor hadn't been gone all that long.

Gone were the filthy carpeting and stained leather seats Nielsen had pictured, replaced by alternating rows of rockers and long tables. The walls were lined with video games and the front with concession stands bereft of soda fountains, candies, and popcorn. Thousands of dollars' worth of arcade furnishings stood around him like technopagan statuary, slabs of dead circuitry haunted by legacies of lost youth. And beneath the hardware, energies remained from an era when secrets of the flesh flickered across the big screen with the same hurrah as an Academy Award winner (even more so, if his father had performed under this very roof); or so he told himself, moving toward the front row.

His left fingers itched under Rae's fresh bandages as he swept his lantern around the room.

His animal instinct was on full alert, now. Come what may—

vermin, safety hazards, inhospitable hosts roused from nests of dirty needles—the "adventurous investigator" in him wanted to blaze his light into every nook and cranny of this former hub of hedonism with its dank chill and gilded plaster-work going to ruin. Raising his lantern to examine the balcony—more video games—he realized he might have spared his wife much suffering if he had taken up urban exploring instead of online cheating... but he mustn't get sidetracked. Another police siren wailed nearby; he waited for it to die down, a lump in his throat.

Finally, he went to the projection screen and set down his equipment. From the backpack he pulled out a black marker, a printout, and a jar. He sank to one knee, picked up the marker and copied the symbol on his paper onto the screen. Then he opened the jar, splashed its contents onto the screen and examined his artwork. It looked close to the Internet image he'd printed: The glyph of *Nagmalitong Yawa Sinagmaling Diwata*, Visayan goddess of lust and seduction. Splattered with his mixture of toilet water and dark, fuzzy specks, his sigil took on a grainy appearance like an old film leader countdown. So weird, he thought... Rae's sloughed-off cancer cells and bacterial growth pasted on a projection screen. But the night's grotesquerie was only beginning.

Time for the ritual he had chosen for the Picante.

Nielsen got to his feet and closed his eyes. The first thing to do was clear the questions buzzing in his mind. How would Rae feel if she knew he'd collected her toilet residue? What if violent squatters lurked nearby? What if a security guard caught him literally with his pants down ("I know what this looks like, sir, but I'm activating a sigil...")? And what about this goddess he wanted to pull into his mind? Was she an actual entity, or a concept or category? Was all this another desperate attempt to create an illusion of control? So much simpler to toss a scrap of paper into a crowd, like his father.

He opened his eyes. For God's sake, he told himself, you're in an old porn theater, you won't be the first to let it all hang out here.

He unzipped his fly.

———

HAVING FORGOTTEN LUBE, Nielsen soldiered on with his activation ritual. Soon a "mature" simulation, a Filipino *Deep Throat* starring Barbara Perez lookalikes, lit up on the projection screen of his mind. Inevitably, Polaroid memories of his mother threatened to ruin the fantasy. But he forced himself to project his shame onto his semi-erect shaft, riding his Oedipal anxiety on a sea of energy formed by everyone who had sat and sweated in the vanished seats behind him.

The payoff was so intense he almost forgot to open his eyes when his orgasm erupted. Eyes stinging with sweat, he watched his gobs of seed transform the glyph into a summoning... of what, he didn't know. Online, he'd found no anecdotal evidence for the material or psychological effects of invoking *Nagmalitong Yawa Sinagmaling Diwata*.

Would the goddess devour his mind the way she was said to devour men she encountered in the forest? Would she destroy him only to rebirth him into the "the flow of mysterious bioelectricity that mirrors the rhythms of nature," as his father had put it?

He sighed and pulled his underwear over his pitiful, ashy penis. He had completed the ritual; time to let his intention sink into his subconscious. Still, an urge to examine his handiwork rooted him to the spot. Closing his fly, he studied the glyph in the lantern light. Something incomplete about it... of course. He had forgotten the most important part of the ritual—the marriage of blood and pus.

He pulled his butterfly knife from his backpack. Flipping it open, he drew blood from the ball of his left thumb and pressed his sacrificial palm to the glyph.

He stepped back and waited.

Well, what did he expect? The sigil flaring to red brilliance? The theater shaking, raining down plaster and timbers? The floor rupturing and freeing the demonic vapors of Hell? For that matter, why end his ritual with a blood offering? According to the myths, the goddess might want all of him for invocation, flesh, hair, teeth, viscera, urine, gastric juices, spinal fluid...

No, don't question yourself. Believe and it will work.

Returning his paraphernalia to his backpack, Nielsen realized he didn't want to leave the theater now. His mission fulfilled, he felt attached to the cavernous milieu, alone with what he liked to think were the Picante's ghosts. They called to the explorer in him, the seeker of buried pasts, the time-traveling impulse that was all the sensual energy he had left after wandering through the desert of cancer for so long.

Feeling almost tipsy, he fancied plopping down in a rocker, kicking his feet up and watching another hardcore Nasino fantasy: An old-school, whitewashing Amazon jungle flick featuring women like Rae, formidably built and pale as moonlight. The idea made his loins tingle, unusual for having spent himself only moments ago. Maybe he should stay awhile. Perhaps he might absorb what it felt like to watch a skin flick here half a century ago. If he closed his eyes and listened to the silence long enough, perhaps he would hear a jazz quartet playing...

Nielsen turned for one last look at the auditorium.

Not a sound out there—but what a view.

He couldn't make out anyone in the audience, just silhouettes in the folding seats. Motionless in a smoky haze, they looked like a single, sprawling body... a voyeuristic ghost. And they were ghosts, in a sense; they could be nothing more. The scene carried on in silence and faded to black around the edges like a vignette effect. It would have looked static, too, if not for the motion of light from the projection booth and screen behind him.

The sigil, he thought. It's working.

Because of the goddess inside him now, he witnessed this moment from an era when porn meant escape inside a living factory—the independent movie house. When sexually explicit films turned audiences into unconscious energy machines pumping out desire before a wall of illusions. Tired of a futile war, America took refuge in seedy palatial imitations like the

Picante to watch idealized visions of itself fucking as it soaked in its own carcinogens, and, depending on the night, its own body fluids. Amazingly, given the technological transformations since then, this was the age into which Nielsen had been born: A time when television didn't look cinematic and movie screenings didn't feel like extravagant extensions of one's living room.

And so many people he had loved or had wanted to love were alive.

His mother, exploring America; his father, playing suicidal knife games; his grandmother, aunts, uncles, cousins, neighbors, eating lechon—all those dead pigs roasting on spits—and playing music in the rooms of what was now his house with Rae and their incontinent dogs.

A time of elders and harmless myths… when Nielsen feared the boogeyman in his closet, not the one in his wife's rectum and liver.

Tears streamed down his face.

Was this how the goddess would devour him? Through his obsession with lost moments, like pictures dying before his eyes at 24 frames per second on a big screen? Through his abhorrence of the present and terror of the future? Was she mocking or tempting him? Trying to teach him something about the dangers of looking backward?

"Go away," he said.

The audience, the smoke, the film projector light vanished.

Yet light still flickered on the arcade furnishings.

Noises rumbled through the room, animalistic and breathy.

His wounded fingers tingling, he turned back around and gaped at the change in his giant canvas. It was a projection screen again, playing a movie as if the projectionist had run into a bad splice only moments ago. As if the Picante had forgotten its slow fade into oblivion ever since the rise of home video forty years earlier. Not that he believed a movie theater could have a mind of its own, like a mansion or truck stop in a horror movie; this was the goddess's work, speaking to him through a hallucination of a simulation. Or so he hoped. He couldn't possibly hold the power to resurrect a structure of objective reality...

Standing three feet from the shuddering glare, Nielsen felt a burning sensation behind his eyes and stepped back into the aisle.

The "midnight showing" looked less like a feature film than a streaming porn video, continuous footage of a white woman receiving a brown cock in doggy-style position. The shaky camerawork reminded him of the Filipino zombie film he'd watched the other night, the effect of the cameraman doing double duty as the actor. What a magnificent ass, he thought, dying at 24 frames per second on his wall of sigil magic, like some exotic satellite containing a portal to another dimension... one he had visited many times in another life before he became *The Stuffener.*

Like a teenage boy, Nielsen tugged at his crotch, wondering if he could get off again to the bittersweet vision. To be that man on the screen, he thought, squeezing both ass cheeks, slapping that smooth, pale skin...

As if the actor heard him, he moved his right hand into the frame, then the left, the fingers wrapped in blue bandages.

The same bandages Nielsen was wearing.

Screen Nielsen's bandages darkened as his fingers began to bleed.

Nielsen gasped as his fresh scabs broke open.

Heedless of the blood trickling down the back of his hand, Screen Nielsen squeezed Screen Rae's buttocks and sped his thrusts. As his wounds bled, so did Nielsen's—a sexually sympathetic stigmata. At the same time, Nielsen grew hard again, his erection straining against his denim as if he might will himself to climax without manual stimulation. Well, he thought, why not try? Just look at that ass, smooth and untouched by cancer treatment. God knows how long it had been since he and Rae had fucked in that position... or in any position.

Then again, perhaps his arousal was part of the hallucination —the blood trickling down his hand, the blood rushing to his dick, a mockery of his supposed "flow of mysterious bioelectricity," a punchline to a joke known only to the spirit he had invoked. If so, he had no choice but to watch himself fuck his wife in Diwata-style Dolby Digital, at least until he saw what the goddess wanted him to see.

Moving toward the screen with arms outstretched, he simulated Screen Nielsen squeezing Screen Rae's buttocks. He knew how silly he must look. But he couldn't stop himself, couldn't tell the illusion to go away—the goddess had broken his resistance through memories too potent. Perhaps even a particular memory, for his hands moved with the ones onscreen as if reliving the experience. As he pressed them to the cold wall of light, he thought this must really be happening: He had invited something evil into himself that tortured him with his own grief. How far could she degrade him as he begged for release into a life without cancer? A replica of the past where he could love Rae through the very root of his desire, not his skill with suture scissors or bottomless capacity for anxiety?

His lust abated, Nielsen sank to his knees and clawed at the screen. All the heartbreak of the last three years tore through him in long, racking sobs. Like a child to their mother's breast, he pressed his face to his sigil, tears and saliva mingling with the invocation of blood, pus, cancer, and jism.

His mother had abandoned him.

His mother *was* the goddess.

A manifestation of what she represented, anyway, a destroyer of things to come. The Arch Denier of futures—chaos engendered in the ancestral consciousness as a female spirit that lures men from their paths and devours them. No one was safe from her cruelty, however, her power to uplift the heart only to devour it through illusions that beckoned even as they mocked.

As he pined for his mother, he longed for a future with Rae that depended on a miracle; his best hope for tomorrow was to build it from yesterday, to walk into the trap beyond the projection screen.

The goddess meant to claim him tonight, in an analog forest he'd hoped would heal him.

Let her take her best shot; he would give himself to her.

On *his* terms.

"Mom," he said.

With his unbloodied hand, Nielsen wiped tears from his eyes and climbed to his feet. Knowing what he was about to say before the giant porn movie of him and Rae, he chuckled.

"Mom..."

This was harder than he expected. He closed his eyes; an image of Vanessa Templonuevo formed in his mind. Not the archetype, the source of his fantasies and infidelities, but the subject of his Polaroids, smiling as if she felt herself fading into the secondhand memory that contained her, bleached out by a mercy long overdue.

"Mom... I forgive you."

To activate his intention, he visualized the image catching fire. Now the goddess could no longer wield her deadliest weapon against him: A single unmotherly act rewritten into a narrative of inexorable abandonment ever since Rae heard the words, "You have a mass inside you." As if his mother's desertion and his wife's prognosis framed an overarching story of love cut short for no other reason than that the universe, much like the deity, delighted in his sorrow.

With a single utterance, he released both women from his myth of betrayal.

He owed them that mercy.

He owed himself that mercy.

Only by healing his oldest wound could he defeat the demon he had summoned; only through forgiveness would he emerge from the dark of the forest.

And now you can't torture me anymore, Goddess. Not with the pain of rejection. You've toyed with that enough. You've humiliated me, shown me how pathetic and desperate I am to recover what I've lost. But I'm done being your plaything. It's my turn to have fun. I order you to use your powers of illusion to serve me. I command you to erase the barrier between me and the door I opened for you. You're going to help me remember what I've forgotten since Rae was diag- nosed with cancer. You're going to teach me how to love her again with all of my being, no matter what the future holds for us. Without my pain, you're nothing more than a subconscious instruction on how to change my reality. Your simulation will give me new eyes, new flesh... new life.

"New life," he shouted, his voice echoing throughout the auditorium.

He opened his eyes and plunged his bloody hand into the projection screen.

————

THE SMELL HIT NIELSEN FIRST. The stench of pus, necrotic tissue, and sloughed-off tumor cells, a "Greatest Hits" of Rae's open-wound woes. Each odor possessed a fetor unique to its origin and metabolic process. As *The Stuffener*, he knew them all. The nursing-home foulness so often conflated with the closeness of death, tissue degradation that tasted like slow goodbyes… but also the sweeter miasmas like E. coli drainage, a mélange of chemical compounds shrieking in the air like the music of vultures. He had trained himself to recognize such smells and focus on the task at hand. Still, their reprise here angered him; if the goddess meant to betray him, he'd sat with them in too many emergency rooms and even the confines of his car when the ER was full to lose his sense of purpose in some disturbing flashback.

Clearly, his catharsis had done nothing to gain the servitude of *Nagmalitong Yawa Sinagmaling Diwata*; she meant to devour him through a different simulation than the one he had in mind.

All right, bring it on, bitch—you can't scare me more than cancer.

But what sort of illusion was this? It looked like a subterranean nightclub designed by Salvador Dali.

A glance over his shoulder showed him the portal was gone, only darkness behind him. Ahead, at the tunnel mouth, a chamber riddled with holes and lit by glowing green streaks that clustered and dispersed like a thermal image of an ant colony. As he emerged from the tunnel, he realized the walls of the vaulted chamber resembled ravaged human skin and the lighting was the product of bioluminescent spiders as large as well-fed rats:

Putrefying wounds and mutated creepy-crawlies, a one-two phobia combo.

For a moment, he wanted to scream like a child lost in a funhouse. His arrogance had led him into this trap; he was certain he would pay for it, as he had paid for every day that he had not begged Rae to see a doctor after her symptoms started. Then he realized the goddess had tapped into another one of his weak points: *Guilt*. As if supporting his wife's decisions about her body made him responsible for her tribulations. And then for the third time that night, fear gave way to animal instinct, or anger overcame his panic: Rae would abhor her illness distorted into this travesty of a Surrealist nightmare.

He moved toward the nearest cavern wall. The clicking glow sticks retreated in all directions, the slower ones crunching and spurting black blood underfoot. Reminding himself that he was not in physical danger, he turned his attention to the holes in front of him. Some were as small as belly buttons, others large enough to poke his head into. Through some cavities, he saw a passageway of subcutaneous fat; through others, an identical chamber on the other side.

He stopped at one wound in particular. The hole was roughly heart-shaped and as big as his van's windshield. The edges around it were bright red, and a tattered strand of skin bisected it diagonally, candle wick-thin at its upper connecting point. Every wound told a story: This one, exaggerated from his memories, had occurred after ulceration caused by radiation therapy. The ulcers had merged into a single wound, the exposed fat underneath covered in sloughy yellow tissue—necrosis.

Nielsen choked back a sob. The slightest tension on the skin strand and it would tear like a chapped lip, ruining any fantasy that the wound counted as two minor holes and not as one gaping atrocity to his wife's flesh, as if that should make a difference—although it mattered to him in the real world, any game that helped him to reduce Rae's traumas in his mind. For all his clinical detachment, he was still a lonely child in the shell of a man who loathed cancer as he would loathe a sexual predator, a rapist with a vampire's thirst.

He clenched his fists.

No. This is not real. Fuck you, Goddess.

She had nearly broken him down again. Tricked him into forgetting this simulation was an abstract pattern, a scrambling of the Biblical torment he tried not to imagine when he nursed Rae's wounds: A kind of sigil. Or… how had his father put it? *An intention-setting amplifier.* With the right mindset, the magical device could be modified to serve his purpose. In this cold, damp underworld thriving on rot, his horror of Rae's wounds could be transmuted into carnal energy, a regenerated capacity to love his partner with all his nerves aflame, to burn with her all the way to the end, however long that took.

As Rae said about therapeutic massage, skin was a medium of loving touch…

Like a toxic messenger from far down in its depths, a spider scuttled from the cavity, breaking the bisecting strand. Shaking off his revulsion, he stared into the yawning tunnel of ribbed, yellowish tissue and imagined a giant vaginal canal, the walls engorged with blood and slick with glandular secretions, a succulent tragedy remade from illness and surgery. He extended his injured hand into the lesion. The nerves in his itching finger-tips collapsed time into one slow, tearful caress as he recalled the first time Rae let him touch her between her thighs so many years ago. Bleeding through his bandages now, his pain pressed to hers, their damaged tissues joining like evolutionary successors of obsolete genital organs… their love growing stronger than ever, built on anguish and X-rays and tumors…

A splashing sound somewhere behind him; he pulled his arm from the hole.

He turned toward the noises. Not ten paces away, his wife pulled herself up from an opening in the floor, nude and bathed in a slime of malignancy and bacterial infection. Her black, lidless eyes shed tears of dead white blood cells as she walked toward him. Not since before her diagnosis had he gazed upon her so intently, taking her all in, the oncologist's sorcery carved into her like ritual mutilations: Cybernetic runes of chemo-therapy and colostomy, transdermal plastics and abdominal wall swelling with parastomal herniation, the diverted colon in her left side leaking mucus and runny shit—Rae like a monstrous rebirth of the affliction trying to kill her, a medically scarified, excremental succubus. Yet all he could think about was their second kiss, when she had crossed the room and pressed her mouth to his with such force that he felt she might really suck the life from him—a memory that never failed to move him.

And his groin tingled as she stood before him now, his bride anew in a dress of exudate and metastatic ichor. The goddess had erred if she hoped to break him down again, for he had never seen Rae so heroic, so strong, so magnificent as she looked in her green-lit gown of slime and sickness, piercing him with her jet-black, pus-encrusted eyes. The decades slammed back in reverse as she mashed her lips against his, fusing him to her in a premonition of parting, a privilege and curse only the sick and their partner can know. Kissing her, drinking her infected tears, he felt inevitability enclose them like a chrysalis, their sorrows, regrets, and panics engulfing them.

Then he realized the encumbrance was not from despair, but mutant spiders. Sharp, burning sensations spread throughout his body. They stung like antiseptic at first, then ravaged his nerve endings like a chemical experiment gone horribly wrong. *Venom.* No stranger to cobwebs brushing his face, he recognized the gauzy feeling of fibers clinging to him like corrosive plastic wrap, paralyzing him in agony as the toxic silk ate through his hair and clothes and skin, encasing him in a final marital embrace, digesting him in love and poison—a sort of chrysalis, after all.

Not the metamorphosis he had asked for.

I've failed. I'm not getting out of the forest tonight. I'm sorry, Rae... goodbye.

Maybe it wasn't all that bad though, dying with this phantom Rae in a romantic tragedy for the horror-convention crowd. Romeo and Juliet hit middle age only to melt into each other in an alien spider-cave of abscess pools and cancerous lesions. For a marriage of blood and pus, a fitting, if extravagant, way to go. But then… who would take care of Rae, the real Rae? Who would nurse her wounds? How would she push on through the desert of cancer without him? How unlike him to succumb readily to a mortal enemy in any world… earthly or etheric… too much hatred ran through his veins! Not just his personal grudges, but the vengefulness of his people after centuries of invasion and colonization, what the goddess was doing with his mind. She had even penetrated a corner of his imagination he dared not visit: The forbidden chamber where his wife waited for him, wasted from treatments and ready to surrender, eager to kiss him goodbye.

Treacherous bitch, the goddess. *Nagmalitong Yawa Sinagmaling Diwata* was like cancer itself—an uncontrolled growth without conscience inside him. But he was inside her, too. And his ability to think, to reason within her sensory construct, meant he engaged with it in a lucid state, aware and purposeful, with the potential to strike back.

But how? Phantom Rae all but suffocated him as the venom threatened to reduce their nuptial kiss to a puddle of gore and slime. He couldn't even cry out.

He needed help. What did he have to work with? He thought of the ghostly audience the goddess had shown him in her first illusion. Patrons from a time when he had depended on his elders, vanished voyeurs who had left their imprint on the Picante, or as his father had put it, *"the energy of a great many people, not necessarily living ones…"*

Please, give me the strength to get out of this, Rae needs me, I can't die tonight—

And then, as if with its own mind, his right hand twitched. Pulled his red-hot butterfly knife from his shredded pants pocket. Three cramped flicks of the wrist and he was sawing through the deadly webbing, pushing Phantom Rae off with his free hand, clambering through the tattered silk. His vision blurry, he staggered away from the apparition and collided with the nearest wall. As he pressed his bandaged fingers to it, his heart thudded in his rib cage like a war drum—miraculously, his pain was subsiding.

If Nielsen had found one advantage since his tumble into the spirit realm, it was situational awareness. He'd become a kind of first-person shooter in the goddess's video game, information updates guiding him like transparent displays transmitted from his subconscious. Right now, his intuition told him the ones who came before him had answered his prayer and put freedom —and vengeance—within his grasp. Even better, his father numbered among the rescuers: His hand belonged to Nestor Nasino now, flipping the knife point-down and attacking the wall with speed and fluidity, playing five finger fillet with the simulation—a parental kindness long overdue.

As if sensing the tide had turned, the eight-legged mutants swarmed over Nielsen and stung every inch of him. Their venom spread harmlessly over his ragged clothes and smoking skin, proof beyond doubt that he had emerged from the chrysalis of despair into a state of balance beyond his adversary's control. Nothing in her illusion, not poison, not heat, not even the acid-drenched metal in his father's hand, could injure him any further. For as long as he remained in her vision of his personal hell, he wielded absolute power to shape it to his needs, limited only by what he could conjure from emotion, memory, imagination.

After everything he had endured tonight, he could imagine a lot.

He imagined his damaged tissues repairing. He imagined himself inflicting pain like a sadist in a torture-porn film, his body a punishing instrument more toxic than an ocean of mutant spider venom. Now *he* was the one devouring the deity. All his anger, fear, sadness, hopelessness, combined to form a ravenous poison for which there was neither antidote nor hope of escape, not even for a vicious demoness, not in *his* illusion, his vision of *her* personal hell. With each knife strike, *Nagmalitong Yawa Sinagmaling Diwata*, devourer of the unsuspecting, fed him her flesh, her being, until, at last, she died screaming in the acid burn of a hex written long before his earliest impulse to kill, a retribution fortified by centuries of practice in the ugliest corners of Filipino magic, by the murderous loathing handed down to him from his forebears and thrust upon him by cancer, a loathing that turned to joy as he tore away the flesh he had mutilated with a dead man's hand.

Then the cave went dark and the weight of rat-sized things lifted from him. The spiders fell into a heap around his feet, the chamber nothing more now than a vacant crypt for a vanquished goddess. His breaths slowed and silk-laced sweat ran into his eyes. The sticky droplets reminded him of Phantom Rae's tears as he wiped them clear, and he thought of the apparition he had left behind in the darkness. Peering into the hole he had made, he made out the theater seats lit dimly by his lantern on the other side. *Freedom*. Still, he would have to cut into the wall again to step back into reality, and he was so very tired.

All the power of his hatred had drained away from him, absorbed into the dead illusion. His legs buckled. He flexed his toes and squeezed his forehead to keep from blacking out.

For fuck's sake, get out of this place... Rae's butt won't stuff itself.

Where had *that* thought come from? He laughed.

And he was still laughing when They reached through the hole and steadied him. He laughed and sobbed and laughed again as invisible limbs wrapped around his armpits and waist and pulled him through the wound-window into the auditorium. His belly ached and his eyes stung from the paroxysms of emotion… pain he'd locked away to shoulder his war against malignancy, the stress crushing every neuron in his tensed body. No time for weakness on the battlefield, no matter how vehemently Rae told him to stop catastrophizing.

Now though, he realized his mindset had merely shielded him from his deepest feelings. Borne along by the past, suspended like a swimmer in dead man's float, he surged with strength to release his pain, emboldened by the ghostly crowd bearing him up the aisle toward an uncertain future.

You are not alone.

The inner voice was not his.

It was Theirs.

He felt like a child again, safe, supported... human. Still laughing, weeping, all the tension ebbing from him into the energy field holding him up. His right hand relaxed, and the butterfly knife slipped from his grasp.

He lost consciousness halfway up the aisle. Then a wash of electronic hysteria roused him, monitors glowing, manic melodies cascading over robotic cacophonies, the arcade games firing up as if they had never stopped playing, a frenzied farewell before excavators claimed the theater and the dread of widowerhood resumed like paper cuts to his nerves again, life in the desert of cancer as usual. Only this time, he told himself, he would try to see past Rae's affliction instead of obsessing with her tumors. The thought would have lulled him to sleep but for the sonic blitz from the ground floor and balcony, and the blurry impression of orange light reflecting off the folding seats, so fleeting he dismissed it as a kind of electro-mechanical mirage. Struggling to remain conscious, he rode the energy field through the archway, across the darkened lobby, and toward the front doors spray painted with vandals' sigils. Locks and chains gave way like silken wisps, and the street spread before him and the zing of impending rainfall filled his nostrils. As if handling an infant, They settled him into a seated position against the building façade and secured the doors.

He passed out again. When he opened his eyes, a car pulled up to the curb and a darkly dressed woman stepped from the driver's seat. She came around the front of the vehicle, one hand hovering near her hip, a stance that made him want to turn his palms up and freeze even though he fought to keep his head from drooping. As she stepped onto the sidewalk, she eased her hand off her gun grip.

"Sir, are you okay," she said.

"Okay," he said.

"Do you require medical assistance?"

"I don't think so, Officer... no."

"You look like you need help. What's your name?"

"It's not a crime to be Filipino."

He sobbed.

"Please, sir, try to remain calm. I'm going to get you help."

Looming over him, the policewoman pulled out her cell phone and dialed 9-1-1.

As he watched her, he thought she looked like Barbara Perez, the "Audrey Hepburn of the Philippines," around the eyes.

"I've had all the help I need," he whispered.

Before he could add, "But thank you," he blacked out.

————

THE NEXT DAY, Nielsen awoke to the sight of his wife standing next to his overbed table, sipping from a box of fruit juice. They waited while a nurse took his vitals and another nurse gave him water and graham crackers.

A doctor came in, inspected his foot dressing, and told him he could leave in an hour.

"You realize," Rae said after the woman had left, "we're going to have to take turns dressing each other's wounds for the next month."

"Sorry," he said.

"Your foot and my butt. What is the universe telling us?"

"I really have no idea how I burnt my foot."

"Apparently, you came in contact with some sort of chemical."

She set down the box of fruit juice and squeezed his knee.

"I won't even ask you, Nielsen, what you were doing in an abandoned porn theater."

"I—yeah. Um…"

"And I won't even ask you how a movie screen can go up in flames without damaging anything else and leave nothing but a handful of ash. That's what the police lady said, anyway. Hopefully, they'll let you off easy because of my cancer. You're welcome."

————

SURE ENOUGH, no one pressed charges against Nielsen, either for trespassing or property damage that defied explanation. He went back to cleaning up dog poop and playing *The Stuffener*. Twice a day, Rae dressed his foot after he stuffed her surgical incisions and ulcers.

He wasn't feeling so good the day a construction crew razed the Picante to the ground.

By nightfall, his burn wound began to ooze green pus and his temperature climbed to 102 degrees. Rae rushed him to the Emergency Room in the musty box he called their "medical frigate," Notorious B.I.G. contemplating suicide on the stereo while she fought the urge to interrogate her husband about his mysterious night at the porn-opera. After the triage nurse called Nielsen away, she took the only choice of seat in the waiting area, a plastic torture device that made her nerve pain feel like sharp fingernails clawing at a sunburn inside her buttocks. She was used to angry wounds though, whereas Nielsen wasn't; she hoped he would get through this setback all right.

It was only fair he should find some peace after everything they had endured in places like the ER, bright, crowded, and ripe with the smell of worry and disease. Although—not that she would ever ask him, no matter how badly she wanted to understand—what made him think he would find anything but trouble breaking into an abandoned porn theater?

She watched the door he'd gone through, thinking, *He's a weirdo, but he's my weirdo.*

Besides—you work with what you've got.

THE REASSIGNED
JO QUENELL

WHEN THE BOYS arrived to take Esme from the cell, she assumed they'd kill her. Yet when they removed the sack from her head she found herself not in a slaughterhouse, but a theater. It was a gaudy old place. Chipped gold trim lined its balconies, and the worn cushions on the unrestored seats held the stench of age. A stage sat before the movie screen, abandoned after celluloid stole the audience's hearts. Now it hosted an empty chair, equipped with restraints and facing the screen.

She didn't fight them. These boys were young, sixteen at oldest. But Esme knew what happened to women like her at the hands of angry young men. She'd read enough about girls found gutted, their remains left in dumpsters and riverbeds. That fear paralyzed her. The prideful woman inside her wilted with shame as she let them lead her onstage and fasten the shackles around her wrists.

The room around her dimmed while the projector lit the screen before her. Esme turned her head, peeking for an exit, anywhere she could run to if given the chance. The redheaded boy to her right grabbed her by the hair and yanked her head back towards the screen. "Watch," he said, the first word she'd heard either boy speak. It was the voice of a child trying to assert himself into something he wasn't. She knew that feeling all too well from a life before. If she wasn't so scared, she may have empathized with him.

Grainy black and white footage danced on screen, lacking sound or credits. The camera faced a man roughly the age of Esme's father, wherever the hell he was. The man sat alone in a room, empty save for the folding table before him. One hand gripped a hammer. The other pinched a nail between his thumb and forefinger, pressing its tip against the table's surface. Without looking, the man brought the hammer down on the nail head with a concentrated, effortless swing. He repeated the action, again and again, never once looking away from the camera, never once breaking his stare with Esme. Once he had hammered the nail through the table, he reached over to pick a new one out of a small pile and begin the process anew. Each swing fell in the same timed, repetitive motion, like he was a machine built to do one thing.

After the man had put a fourth nail through the table, Esme turned to the boy on her left.

"W-what is this?"

"Shut up before we break your fucking jaw," the boy said. His confident tone sent a cold shiver down Esme's spine. She turned back to the screen, fighting the urge to cry.

The man's trance broke after the tenth nail. His gaze shifted offscreen and his brow furrowed. Esme couldn't place what changed in his eyes. His mouth moved, but his words were muted.

Suddenly the screen went black. Esme sat in the darkness, her heavy breathing the only audible sound. She swallowed and waited for one of the boys to slit her throat, leaving her to choke on her blood in the empty theater. But when the lights came on, neither boy brandished a weapon of any sort. Instead, they each unstrapped the restraints securing her to her chair. Esme hadn't realized how bad they'd pinched her skin until her wrists were free.

She barely had the chance to exhale with relief before the boys pulled the sack back over her head.

———

THE SMELL of grime and waste greeted Esme as the boys returned her to her cell. They locked shackles around her wrists and ankles, anchoring her once more to the brick wall, before tearing the sack off her head.

From the other side of the cell, Daniel hocked a loogie in the direction of the guards as they walked back to the barred door. It hit the ground at the feet of the redhead. Neither boy even offered a glance in response.

"Come on," Daniel said. "I dare you. I fucking dare you. Come at me again. Take these cuffs off and make it fair this time. See how long you last."

Judging by the deep bruises blotting his naked body, they'd gotten an advantage on him before. But Daniel didn't break until the guards had left the cell, heading into a hallway awash with the moans and cries of others. Only then did he acknowledge Esme.

"You okay?" he said.

"They didn't hurt me, if that's what you mean." The question itself made her blood boil. Of course she wasn't fucking okay.

Daniel exhaled and rubbed his patchy beard with cuffed hands. "Where'd they take you?"

Esme sat on the cold ground and pulled her legs to her chest, the only act she could think of to block her nudity. "A theater."

Daniel nodded. "Same."

"They showed me something. A film, I guess. I don't know what it was, or the point of it. Honestly, I think I was just relieved they didn't kill me."

"The second I saw that chair, I figured I'd be tortured to death. I could barely pay attention to the...the movie, or whatever you want to call it."

"What do you think it meant? You know, the hammering?"

Daniel frowned. "What hammering?"

"Onscreen. The man hammering nails."

Daniel shook his head. "They must have shown me something different."

"Really?"

"There wasn't any man. Just a lady, wearing a dress out of the fifties or something. Real put together and all that. She looked scared. I dunno, there was just...something in her eyes. She was standing in a kitchen, and kept opening an oven to check in it, then closing it. Over and over again, just opening and closing, for ten minutes straight. Then it ended, and they took me back here. I have no idea what it meant."

Esme stayed quiet. Nothing in the past day made sense. Since coming out she had trained herself to expect the unexpected, knowing each new day could bring an unpleasant twist. But this was all worse than she could ever expect. "Well shit. Why us? What did we do?"

Daniel snorted. "Why us? Hell, look at us." For the first time his eyes fell on Esme's body; not out of desire, but something close to fear. "Pretty clear to me why they chose us. Questions is, what do they plan to do?" He sat down on the dirty floor and rested his head against the brick wall. "Whatever it is, I don't see how it can be any fucking good."

———

THE BOYS TOOK her from the cell again the next day. When they removed the sack from her head, she found herself in a small office. Across from her, in a fashionable gray pantsuit, sat a familiar face.

"I'm glad to see you made it through the first night in one piece," the woman said. "Not everyone does. The restraints typically keep people from making terrible decisions. But some surprise you." Her cold tone curdled Esme's blood. It differed from the warm voice over the phone. But the woman's face matched the photo on the website—striking futures, beauty refined by age. Her wrinkles hinted at inherent wisdom, and behind her glasses, blue eyes held confidence. The woman's professionalism both drew Esme in and petrified her.

"My name is Dr. Rothson," the woman said. "It's not the name I provided you prior, and I apologize for that. Doctor and patient relationships require trust, and I've breached that from the start. Please know that secrecy is crucial to my practice. Moving forward, I promise transparency."

Patient. The word hit Esme with the force of a thrown brick. The woman in the ad wasn't a doctor. She was the vocal coach closest to Esme's neighborhood, and one of the few in her price range. She specialized in helping women like Esme, and her website had seemed to go out of the way to cater to her comforts, using words like *safe space,* boasting that *hate has no place here.*

Esme tried to speak, but her voice shrank into her throat. "What is this?" she finally managed.

"Consider this therapy," Dr. Rothson said.

"I already see a therapist."

"And I'm sure they give you all the positive affirmations you need, correct? Tell me. What in your life have they actually fixed?"

"Nothing in my life is broken," Esme said.

Something crossed Dr. Rothson's face, either a smirk or a scowl. No emotion appeared in her eyes, which remained her captor. "Nothing may be broken. But I see illness. You're sick, and you've been misled to believe otherwise." A sliver of a smile curled the doctor's thin lips. "Fortunately, all sickness can be fought in some way or another."

It wasn't the first time someone had called Esme sick. But nobody ever had the guts to do it to her face. Normally it was some fuckhead screaming out of a car window, or some internet random feeling brave behind their computer screen. Hearing someone say it so matter-of-factly in front of her filled her with more than the usual rage. She considered what Daniel said-- *Pretty clear to me why they'd choose us.* The urge to scream became overwhelming. Instead, she tried swallowing down her fear. And when she opened her mouth, she let loose every expletive she knew, all directed with barbs toward the hag in front of her.

Dr. Rothson sat, unamused, not even flinching at the worst verbal attacks Esme could throw her way. She waited patiently until Esme ran out of breath and gasped for air.

"Did that make you feel better, Elliottt?"

The name caught Esme off guard. It had been years since someone had called her that. She fought off the urge to sob and stared at the ground, refusing to make eye contact with the doctor.

Who the hell told her?

"Your therapy will resume this afternoon," Rothson said. "Afterwards, we will take a blood draw to test its susceptibility. We'll maintain two sessions a day until we start seeing the results we want. After which, we'll scale down to once a day, and taper you off from there. Typically, it takes eight weeks for us to see meaningful results, but ultimately these things vary depending on the patient."

"Transparency," Esme said in a whisper.

Dr. Rothson frowned and cocked her head.

"You told me that going forward you'd use more transparency," Esme said louder, trying to lace her voice with as much venom as she could. "So maybe now's the time to stop being so fucking cryptic."

Dr. Rothson sighed. She removed her glasses and closed her eyes, pinching the bridge of her nose as if fighting off a headache.

She told Esme everything.

———

ESME SCREAMED and fought the boys with everything she had on the way back to her cell.

They were more than ready to fight back.

———

ESME'S next therapy session was delayed until the swelling eased. Until then she remained in a world of mute darkness, her lips too cracked and sore to speak. She listened to the sound of Daniel's strength falter, then break, as his treatments continued. After two days his sobs shifted in pitch, growing higher. Her heart steadily broke for him, but every time she tried comforting him, her lips split open.

By the time she could see again, his physical changes had already started.

She struggled once more when they brought her back to the theater. Her fight diminished fast. The energy wasn't there. The last beating, paired with nothing more to consume than murky water, had broken her will.

The boys dropped her into the seat, then tightened the restraints around her wrists until the buckles bit into her skin. She clamped her eyes shut as the lights went down and the projector started up. The redheaded boy pinched the lobe of her left ear and twisted until she gasped in pain.

The film was the exact same. The tired man lifted the nails and hammered in silence, his weathered eyes staring directly into Esme's. Any time Esme even blinked, one of the boys tugged at her hair or pinched her skin. Soon she stared until tears blurred her vision, afraid to do much else.

After the tenth nail entered the tabletop, the man's gaze again shifted offscreen. And once more his mouth opened, saying something indistinguishable. The expression on his face changed to something Esme couldn't read. The film continued playing past the point where it first cut off, remaining on the man staring offscreen, his brows furrowing.

Under the click of the spinning projector reels, Esme heard something too soft to make out. Something she couldn't place as on the film, in the room, or inside her own head.

A woman's voice.

The film abruptly shut off before she could make sense of it. The projector clicks slowed, then stopped, and the lights switched on. Esme finally blinked and tears ran down her bruised face. The fine hairs on her arms stood. She gasped for air. Hadn't even realized that, at some point, she'd stopped breathing. Her body tensed as she waited for the boys to pull the sack over her head and undo her restraints.

Instead, the redheaded boy reached into a cargo pocket on his pants and pulled out an electric razor.

———

IN HER DREAMS she wasn't naked and restrained, and her long hair hadn't been shaved down to stubble. Daniel no longer occupied the opposite side of the cell. In his place sat the man from the film, stationed in his spot at the table. Esme sat across from him, her palms resting flat against the tabletop. She knew what would happen before he picked up the first nail.

She tried lifting her hands but they stuck to the wood surface. She begged, swearing *I won't tell anyone, please, let me go, I'll do anything.* Yet her words came out muted, incomprehensible, the same frail voice she'd heard on the film.

The man placed the tip of the nail against the back of Esme's right hand, between the knuckles of her pointer and middle finger. Holding it steady was a battle—a steady tremor plagued his grip. Beneath the musk and filth of the cell, Esme smelled stale booze wafting off him. It reminded her of the dreaded childhood trips to her grandparent's, the constant nights where her grandfather would barge through the front door after a night at the VFW, screaming and swearing.

Suddenly everything about the man before her embodied all she had grown to hate about masculinity.

He placed the hammer on the nail head, lining it up. Esme cried as fear, frustration and rage battled to become her dominant emotion. She tried kicking him, but her feet were anchored to the ground. There was no escaping what came next. She closed her eyes but someone behind her grabbed her face, forcing her eyelids back open. All she could do was stare at the man before her.

A single defeating thought crossed into her mind, stinging worse than any blow: *Elliott wouldn't be here.*

The man's opened his mouth to speak, and out spilled the rapid clicking of a projector reel.

He raised the hammer, then slammed it down.

Esme woke with a gasp. She lifted her head, wincing in pain at the start of a brutal headache, and took a moment to orient herself. She still lay naked on the floor of the cell, the shackles on her wrists and ankles secured by chains. A cold, thick sweat moistened the buildup of grime coating her, creating an unpleasant film. On the other side of the cell, Daniel lightly snored, his body turned away from Esme. Since the changes had started, he'd refused to face her. Refused to let anybody but himself see. Esme understood—if everything Dr. Rothson had said was true, her own changes would be starting very soon. It was too dreadful of a thought to even process.

As if on cue, a burning sensation tore across her jawline. Esme touched her chin, then quickly retracted her hand. A sinking pit cratered throughout her gut.

No. It was impossible.

Once a week for nearly two years, Esme had lay still while a technician stabbed her face with a small, sharp probe registering an electric shock that killed each individual hair follicle. Her pain threshold had never been good and the whole thing hurt like shit, but removing her beard growth once and for all had been incredibly affirming. After all the time, money and pain she'd invested, this shouldn't be fucking happening.

Esme touched her face again. A low moan escaped her throat.

Stubble scratched her fingertips.

———

ROTHSON DIDN'T REACT at all in the way Esme hoped. A small smirk curled the side of her mouth as she pulled a kerchief from her blazer pocket, then removed her glasses and wiped the right lens clean. She dabbed the remains of Esme's spit from her cheek, folded her kerchief into a square, and placed it on her desk.

"Let's try that again," Rothson said. "How are you feeling, Elliott?"

Esme shook free the strand of spittle dangling from her lip. She didn't speak. Didn't even raise her head to look at the woman before her. She stared at her right hand, shackled to the arm of her chair. The hairs on her knuckles and forearm were already growing thicker. It had only been a few days since her last hormone doses. Things shouldn't be reverting this fast.

Rothson sighed, then picked a piece of paper from her desk. She studied it a moment before speaking. "Well the positive news is that your testosterone levels have climbed. And it appears that the therapy sessions have sped up the masculinization process."

It was true--horrifically so. Esme had spent the last five years putting herself into debt in order to change her body in ways that aligned with her soul. It had been painful and expensive, with only scarce help from insurance. But it had all been worth it. And now it was disappearing by the day. The jaw which had been surgically contoured into a narrow, feminine shape had become square and pronounced once more. Her eyebrows lost their elevated arch. The hair on her head grew back with a deep recession along the scalp. The stubble on her chin sprouted thicker than even before she started treatments to eliminate it.

"However, your estrogen levels are still far too high. And while your testosterone has risen, it's still much lower than we want. This isn't unexpected for a patient who is post-op. However, this could potentially stall any progress, and that's the last thing we want. I recommend we increase your treatment to three times daily and do another blood draw next week."

Esme stared at the ground and said nothing. Rothson eyed her expectantly. "The floor is yours if there is anything you want to say."

Esme refused to look up. "How do you know me?"

Rothson pondered the question. "Explain."

"My name--the old one. It's been changed for years. How do you know it?"

Rothson cleared her throat. "You can change your name, or alter your appearance however you want. But nothing can ever be completely erased, can it? No matter how deep you bury a body, it can always be dug up."

A pregnant pause filled the room. Rothson's cell phone vibrated on her desk. She checked the text message then nodded to the redhead boy at the door.

"She's here. Please let her in."

The boy opened the door and left. Rothson stood and walked to a closet nestled into the left corner of her office. She extracted a long wool coat and brought it to Esme, draping it over her shoulders. It was the first piece of clothing to touch Esme's skin since this nightmare began. "You have a surprise guest coming. Try to relax. It will make everything feel much easier."

Esme struggled in her chair, trying to knock the scratchy coat off of her. The binds kept her from succeeding. She gave up with a frustrated grunt. "You understand people are going to be looking for me, right? You might think I'm just some sad, lonely tranny that nobody will miss, but I have plenty of people who care about me. They'll figure out where I am, and then you'll rot in a cell."

Another smirk marred Rothson's lips before morphing into a full-fledged smile. The doctor said nothing. Fear fluttered in Esme's chest and she wished more than anything to escape Rothson's stare.

The door behind her opened. Rothson's eyes moved to the newcomer entering the room. The smile disappeared and her cold professionalism returned. "I am so glad you could make it. I hope the trip wasn't too taxing."

Someone murmured, followed by the shuffling of feet. The hairs on Esme's neck stood. The sound of a familiar voice sucked the breath from her lungs.

"My boy."

Esme hadn't spoken to her mother since the first awkward year of transition, when she cut out the people who wouldn't show support. Changing her last name to something out of the bloodline felt like a final 'fuck you' to them all.

But now here she was--the woman who birthed her, raised her, then let her down when she needed her the most. The last five years had not been kind to her. She placed a wrinkled, spotted hand on her daughter's forearm. Esme retracted as much as the bindings would allow. She focused her gaze back onto the floor. Her mother removed her hand abruptly. A muted sob escaped her, filling Esme with a moment of defiant joy.

"He's still coming around," Rothson said. The doctor motioned to a chair beside her desk. "Please, Mary. Sit."

Esme's mother obeyed, slouching into her chair as if the grief caused by Esme's rejection had zapped her of life. Esme couldn't find the words to adequately express her rage.

"Now Elliott," Rothson said. "Part of therapy will be fixing the relationships most damaged by your choices. From several interviews now it seems that your mother is the person you owe the most atonement to."

"I owe her fucking nothing," Esme said.

Her mother let out another pathetic sob. "He never used to treat me like this!" She wept openly, grabbing a handful of tissues from a box on Rothon's desk and wiping streaks of runny mascara from her cheeks.

Esme thought about the week after their last conversation. How her chosen family wouldn't leave her side, worried for her safety. Even once she managed to move past that horrible time, her mother's final words still cut.

"Nobody will see you as anything other than an ugly joke."

She thought of all the rebuttals she could make, but knew it was useless. Anything she could say would get twisted and turned against her. She kept her mouth shut.

"Elliott," Rothson said, "it's important to take this step of remediation now, rather than later when you two are cohabitating again. A healthy support system is crucial for your recovery."

Esme's stomach sank. *"Cohabitate?"*

Something flashed in Rothson's eyes. Glee. She was enjoying every moment of this. "As a licensed mental health expert, I have determined that you are no longer deemed as fit to take care of yourself. Your mother has retained guardianship over you, effective now and continuing after you leave here. Your work, landlord and close acquaintances have been informed that you have moved back home to Montana. And once you leave here, that will be truthful."

Esme's mother raised her hand. "And when should I expect to take him home?"

"At this moment, that is unclear," Rothson said. "While we're seeing magnificent gains, we have a long way to go. Plenty more treatments are needed. But I am confident we will get there sooner rather than later."

Esme may have well been hit. She tried to form words but failed. Rothson folded her hands on her desk and leaned forward, as if daring Esme to spit again. "I'm sure that this is a lot to process at the moment. But please understand that this decision is made with your best interests in mind."

Her mother reached over once more and placed her hand on Esme's arm. "We'll be back together again. Just like we once were. Just like we're supposed to be." She touched Esme's face. "Your room is nearly the exact same. We'll have to change some things--you're not a boy anymore. You need a man's room. It will be ready when you come home." She smiled wide. "I promise."

Esme wanted to knock out her teeth. Wanted to break every bone in her body, then turn her rage onto Rothson. She thrashed in her chair, using every ounce of energy she had to try and break the restraints holding her in place. Esme's mom jumped back in shock, and looked to Rothson with panic.

"He'll tire himself out," Rothson said.

Esme stopped only once her wrists were bleeding and she struggled to catch her breath.

Then she screamed until her voice gave out.

———

"THEY'RE LIARS," Daniel said. "Absolute fucking liars."

His voice had changed to a pitch and cadence that Esme had always wanted but could never quite get. He sat against his dele-gated wall in the cell, legs clamped together, arms folded across his chest. The affirming parts each of them had worked so hard and braved so much to earn had been torn away and swapped. Esme's bosoms had flattened into a surfboard chest while Daniel's had filled out. And while Esme tried to keep her eyes to herself, it became harder not to steal glances at Daniel and feel the same stabs of sad envy that plagued her when she was younger.

She'd caught Daniel giving her the same hopeless looks more than once already.

"All this bullshit they're feeding me, about how they're glad to have their daughter back. How they're coming in with open arms, ready to be a family again. As if they weren't the ones who threw me onto the street when I needed them most." He wiped tears of frustration from his rounded cheeks. "I was 16. Still a kid. Came home from school the day after telling them and found the locks changed on our house, and a duffle bag packed on the front porch. They didn't give me any more than a fifty-dollar bill and a six-pack of Pedialyte. And now they have a space for me in their home? Fuck that. I'll kill them."

Esme simply nodded. She didn't have anything to add. What really was there to say, anyway?

"I'm going to fight," Daniel said. "With everything I have. Next time they take me out of here. I won't stop until one of us isn't moving. It's them or me." Despite his changing features, one thing remained the same--the rage in his eyes. "I'm getting out of here, one way or another."

But despite Daniel's boasting, his fight never seemed to come. Every day they took him for his treatments, and every day he came back looking a bit more broken than before. And Esme's own time in the theater grew longer. The film itself had extended into a monotonous director's cut--the nail pile beside the man had grown in mass, and now instead of ten minutes Esme spent a half hour, three times a day, watching him hammer them into the table. Nothing else changed about the film. At the end of every session, his glance would move offscreen and the reel ended with him mouthing silent words. Then her captors would pull the sack over her head and bring her back into the cell, swapping her for Daniel.

When the boys came into the cell one day, the redhead threw a set of clothes at Esme's feet. "Get dressed," he said, unlocking her shackles. Esme stood and picked the clothes up off the ground. The scratchy flannel shirt fit loose over her now flat chest, and she had to hold the corduroy pants up. After days--or weeks, or months, she couldn't tell anymore--spent naked, the clothing felt awkward. When they led her from the cell, they no longer restrained her or covered her head with a sack. One guard stayed in front of her and the other behind as they walked through the guts of a prison, each side of the hallway lined with cells similar to the one Esme occupied. Through the corners of her vision, Esme eyed the emaciated, tortured bodies of those like her. She wondered just how many souls had been put through this, and what ever became of them.

She kept her eyes out for an exit. Something she could dash toward when given the chance. But no such doorway existed from her cell to the theater. Everything was concrete walls and iron bars, off which the cries of victims echoed.

————

SHE RETURNED from her night session to an empty cell. Daniel was nowhere to be seen; hell, even the shackles that had held him in place had been removed. A blank brick wall faced Esme, and for the first time in however long she had been in this cell, she sat in silence.

She stayed awake throughout the night, awaiting Daniel's return. But the cell door never opened. She remained alone. Her own thoughts raced. Did he fight like he said he would? The possibility made her stomach ache. Daniel was resilient. She knew that. But she didn't have faith that he could win in a fight. Not after the lack of food, the lack of sleep. Their spirits were being broken, and it was cracking them into bits. Esme lowered her head. She was becoming resigned to her fate.

For better or worse, she was growing to accept it.

————

DR. ROTHSON'S face stayed as steely and emotionless as ever. "It is not ethical to discuss another patient with you. How would you like me to share your confidential information with others?"

"Ethics seem really important to you. Cool. Great." Esme had stopped trying to speak with a feminine lilt. Keeping it up had grown too hard. "I just want to know if he's still alive. That's all."

"All you need to know is that Ms. Lafferty is receiving the correct services needed to overcome her ailments," Dr. Rothson said. "At this point in your treatments, it is no longer appropriate to keep you both in the same cell. For your well-being, and her safety."

The implication of Rothson's comment hit Esme in the gut. She tried to think of a response, but came up short. It was wrong. Just so wrong.

Before she had started on her journey of self-realization, Esme had slept with only two women. For a long time, she assumed it was something wrong with her. She didn't feel the desire to play the game, or to treat women like they belonged to her. It took coming out and changing into her correct form to realize how it was more complex than that. Whatever Rothson claimed of her had no ground in reality.

Or did it?

Esme thought of moments in the cell, watching Daniel's changes from the corners of her eyes. The way he softened, his body shifting towards a delicate feminine shape. The way something spun inside of her when she caught a flash of the fold between his legs. No matter how quickly they fled, she'd had shameful thoughts. The type she'd never remembered having before, even before transition.

Her face burnt with shame. Esme lowered her head, but couldn't escape Rothson's assertive gaze. "You keep fighting, Elliott," the doctor said. "And I appreciate you. But your time is nearly up. Your treatment is nearly over." She looked over her notes and nodded to herself. "You are scheduled for three more therapy sessions, and will then complete your exit interview. Depending on your performance there, you will shift to outpatient services." Something nearing compassion crossed Rothson's face and somehow it was more terrifying than her typical stone demeanor. "It can be hard to leave a center such as this and return to life. I understand that there might be difficult feelings related to this change in placement. That is why it's important for us to start setting up support. I have made referrals to some wonderful doctors in Montana who will continue providing you care. And if anything happens, they will contact me immediately. It's rare, but resuming intensive therapy is an option if needed. Any questions so far?"

"How does it feel to lose?" Esme said.

Rothson's demeanor shifted again. Esme couldn't read it. She didn't care to. "Nothing you have done has changed me. Not in a way that can't be fixed. You think that sending me back to square one has defeated me? Maybe made me decide I've been wrong my whole life? That I'm actually a guy? Change my features all you want. You haven't changed me. I can leave here and start again. Then I'll come back and tear your fucking heart out."

Rothson smirked. She opened a drawer on her desk and removed a hand mirror, which she turned to face Esme.

She'd known what she'd see would be horrid. It was worse than what she expected. Her beard had grown in course and speckled with gray, and her hairline receded into a deep arch reaching the back of her head. Neither of these things were surprises. But what shocked her was the gray dishwater color of her skin, and the way it sagged on her face. She had aged twenty years in a matter of days. She remembered taking a history class in college and seeing photos of coal miners in the early days of industrialism; how harsh work turned young men into fragile shells. That was what she saw staring back at her.

"There's no changing back, Elliott," Rothson said. "This is you. The real you. Something inside of you has been activated. Something that's been in there all along. Believe it or not, but your bullishness is slipping. By the end of your therapy sessions, you will embrace it." She put down the mirror and stood from her desk, stepping toward Esme. "I've seen so many like you fight even harder until the last second. But my methods are foolproof. By the time you leave here, you will have embraced your true form. I believe it with all my heart." Rothson approached Esme, reached out, and grabbed her face. Nails dug into Esme's cheeks as the doctor pulled her face close. Hot, rank breath slapped her. Esme noticed the mottled, blanched skin hidden poorly under layers of caked foundation and concealer, and the slight jaundiced tint in the whites of Rothson's eyes. The doctor had been terrifying when flawlessly put together. But the sights of her imperfections made her even worse.

"I believe in you, Elliott," Rothson said, pushing her face towards Esme's until they were close enough to kiss. "I believe in you. I believe in you. I believe in you."

Esme could taste her awful breath and it was enough to make her gag. But she didn't fight it. Something, be it fear or resignation, kept her compliant.

"I believe in you," Rothson repeated, and the joy cracking her voice was the worst thing Esme had ever heard. "I believe in you. I believe in you. I believe in you. I believe in you."

———

IT WAS ONLY when Esme returned to her cell and closed the gate that she realized nobody had escorted her. She had made the walk from her final therapy session back to the prison without anybody keeping watch, squandering her one chance to escape. She should have been upset, but instead she just felt tired. She looked forward to sleep and peace. It had been days since she had last seen Daniel, but she'd grown to appreciate the quiet of her lone cell. Esme laid down on the center of the cell floor, grateful to be free of the shackles. She closed her eyes, embracing the best sleep of her life.

———

SHE AWOKE to something squirming inside her; writhing near her pelvis before slithering downward. Pain ripped through her —this must have been what giving birth felt like. The thing, whatever it was, pushed between her lower lips. Esme felt a deep strike of panic. She quickly undid the pants belted around her waist and yanked them down.

Whatever she saw between her legs gave her pause.

It had been over two years since the surgery. Two years since she had taken away the thing that haunted her most; the thing that kept her from moving forward from her former life. The process had been hell, putting her into a debt she was unsure she'd ever recover from. But goddamn, by taking it away she felt closer than ever to embracing her true self.

Now something new grew in place.

It didn't resemble her former genitalia. Hell, it didn't look like any sort of human organ. A hard, scaled outer shell coated its worming body, adorned with rows of jagged barbs slicked with her blood. At the top, a long, curved hook curled towards her. The thing stretched out of her, five inches, then eight, ebbing and flowing in and out of her body.

The pain was madness. Her labial lips hung in tatters, and a mess of gore pooled beneath her. If the agony wasn't enough to make her pass out, then surely the horror of seeing her new organ should.

Yet she didn't feel fear seeing it. She didn't know what she felt. Despite the pain, a lackadaisical smog clouded over any sort of dominant emotion. She could place it as the same sort of gray haze that haunted her before she began to transition. The feeling she most equated with being a man was back, and stronger than ever.

The cell filled with the sound of a hammer hitting a nail.

She didn't need to turn her head far to see him in the corner. A sickly, jaundiced glow emanated from the man's flesh, filling the room with piss-yellow light. He sat, hammering nails into the table, just like always. Esme wasn't scared to see him. She didn't feel anything.

The man faced Esme. A nail fell from between his fingers, clattering against the table. He stood abruptly, sending his chair to the ground. His mouth fell ajar, and out spilled the click of a film reel winding from its spool. Esme heard his words, and understood them. Fighting through the pain coursing through her pelvis, she slowly arose from the cell floor.

The man stepped towards her, leaving the nails behind but

gripping the hammer. His gait was slow, and he walked with a slight limp. He stopped before Esme, leaving a foot of distance between them. She'd assumed he'd be taller than her, but they stood eye to eye. Odors wafted off of him and they reminded her of her grandfather--old spice failing to cover up stale whiskey. Instead of repulsing her, they felt like home.

The two stared into each other's eyes for what felt like ages, but must have been only a minute. The man broke the stare, then stepped back. He swung the hammer upward with a shocking force. There was a sickening crack as the claws tore into his scalp. If he felt pain, he didn't show it; didn't even flinch. He pulled the hammer free, and a glut of dark blood spilled from dual holes, accompanied by the flatulent whistle of compressed air leaving his skull. He held the hammer out to Esme, who took it with a shaking hand. He then reached into the holes with hooked pointer fingers and yanked. The sound reminded Esme of someone trying to tear wet wallpaper. He tugged the skin of his face lower, exposing muscle and gore. Blood slicked his hands and spattered against the floor in a steady stream. The flesh tore free once reaching his mouth, leaving only a wet flap dangling off his chin. He turned the ragged tatters of his face in his hands and held it up to Esme, lining the raw, dripping side up with her features. Then he pushed it against her skin, pressing firmly. Warm pockets of fat and sinew mashed against Esme's skin. She could smell coppery blood and something indescribably foul. Yet she accepted it. And when the man removed his hands, she offered hers to keep his face in place.

Blood dripped into Esme's eyes, blurring her vision. The thing between her legs extended further and further out. She felt like she was falling down a well, far from the room and into some foreign place. Something inside of her broke into a million pieces, and with a sense of indifference, she swept them all away.

Before she slipped completely into the void, she watched the man take the hammer once more. With another concentrated swing, he drove the claws into his eye.

———

H<small>E AWOKE</small> to the sound of the cell doors opening. Sat up, wiped sleep from his eyes. His head rang with a sharp pain, like he was coming off a beast of a bender.

The air stank of blood and decay, but save for a few damp spots on the floor, the cell was spotless.

A familiar figure stood at the door, accompanied by the two young men he'd come to know as his escorts. "It's time for your exit interview, Elliottt," Rothson said from the doorway, as cold as ever. Even yesterday, her voice would fill him with venomous spite. But now he felt nothing. Absolutely nothing.

Elliottt stood, wiping his hands on the seat of his pants and picking the hammer from the ground. Its handle was wet and red. He tucked it into a loop on his pants and followed Rothson out of the cell.

The theater was full for the first time. Bodies dressed in nice clothes occupied every seat in the house. They turned as Dr. Rothson led Elliottt through the entrance, staring at him through the sockets of blank, genderless masks. As Rothson brought Elliottt onstage, one of the blank-faced spectators in the front row pulled their mask down for a brief moment. Elliottt's mother beamed at her son before covering up once more.

The screen was gone, as was the restraining chair. A simple card table and folding chair sat in its place. Rothson gestured towards the setup and Elliottt took a seat. Rothson left him onstage, taking a spot next to Elliottt's mother in the front row.

Elliottt looked to the pile of nails resting on the left side of the table. He picked one up, lined its tip against the table, and pulled the hammer from its loop. He pounded the first nail into the table, then picked up the next. He did not need to think about the process, or question why he was doing it. He just knew.

The audience watched with their blank faces. Nobody moved. Nobody even breathed. Elliottt starred in this show. Nobody else here mattered. It gave him a sense of purpose like he had never previously known. He hammered the next nail harder.

Something crashed offstage after he finished with the tenth

nail. His eyes darted from the task at hand to the disturbance. His face blanched with rage as he gripped his hammer and clenched his jaw, ready to punish whoever would distract him from his work.

A woman walked out, clutching her right hand. A burn covered her palm, already blistering. Black mascara trails webbed her cheeks. She stepped towards him on shaky legs, clearly in need but cautious to get too close. He smelled something; food burning. He understood it to be an inconvenience, one that was all her fault.

She had to pay for that.

Something else flashed in his mind. He knew her from somewhere else; a place in the past muddled by clouds of smog. A name passed by him--*Daniel*--and for a split moment he did not feel rage, but instead sadness. His grip on the hammer eased.

Then she opened her mouth, and a horrible mechanical whine spilled out. It was the sound of breakage, of film being stretched and torn apart by machinery. It pierced his eardrums and he wished for deafness over ever having to hear it again. Any feeling other than anger left and he stormed from the table, sending his chair clattering against the stage.

He would shut her up for good.

The first hammer blow sent her to the ground, and for a moment he thought that was all it would take. She went quiet for a moment, stunned by the abrupt pain. She grabbed at her cheek, trying to staunch the blood seeping out of split skin. Then she opened her mouth and the horrible shriek came out again, louder. He kicked her onto her back and swung again. The next blow splintered her eye socket. The following jellied her eye. Her screaming only increased so he focused his rage on her mouth, swinging until her teeth were shards and her jaw was broken.

He stepped back once her screams had become the labored whine of a dying animal, and surveyed his work. She lay on her back, head rocking back and forth. Any resemblance to someone from his past had been destroyed. Gore caked her face and puddled on the stage beneath her. The remains of her right eyeball hung out of its ruined socket, dripping fluid and slime. Her lips quivered, unable to form words.

The audience watched it all, stone silent.

He noticed her skirt, ridden up and showing him the world. She wasn't wearing panties. Something spun in his stomach, and the thing in his pelvis once again slithered out between his legs, its barbs further catching and tearing the folds made in his previous life, and it hurt but sometimes pain is welcome. The thing grew and writhed in his pants and he stared at the woman on the ground and knew, in the end, she wasn't a burden but a reward, and he was ready to claim his prize.

He set down the hammer and unbuttoned his pants.

NOSTALGIA NIGHT AT THE SNUFF PALACE

BRENDAN VIDITO

1

THERE WERE FOUR OF THEM—BRIAN, Katy, Armaan, and Geoff—trudging through the ruins of the city like living nuclear shadows. Winter garments caked with ash and grime hung in tatters over their emaciated frames. Exhaustion chiseled deep lines their faces, and blue, bleeding lips whispered lyrics to half-forgotten songs—a futile attempt to soften the horror of their surroundings. They were close now. Once they reached the heart of the city, and the miraculously still-standing movie palace, their pilgrimage would be complete.

Cresting a hill formed by shattered concrete and rusted rebar, the pilgrims approached a ruined gas station and collapsed into the dirt. The metal canopy leaned at an angle, one end raised toward the sunless cauldron of the sky. Shadows congregated underneath, thick as pitch. With cautious glances, the pilgrims ensured they were a safe distance away. The darkness likely held the hungry, the desperate, or the deranged. Worse still, it could be concealing one of them—the so-called Carolith—their bodies sleek, unmoving, and indistinguishable from shadow. Unlike the threat of physical violence, there would be no chance of surviving an encounter with the Carolith. And so the pilgrims kept a wary distance, watchful in spite of their debility.

Geoff removed his backpack with painful, meticulous movements. The zipper had long since broken and the opening was held together with safety pins. He removed one of them with blistered fingers, reached inside, and removed a shapeless thing wrapped in soggy newspaper. A blurred headline hinted at a war remembered now as a distant, collective nightmare. The stink emanating from it was so powerful, so nauseating, it seemed to extend putrid, fecal-stained fingers into the nostrils and down the throats of the pilgrims. Despite their revulsion, saliva sprang into their mouths. They drew nearer as Geoff peeled away the newspaper membrane—matted fur oleaginous with brown, clotted blood, the bright flash of bone. It was so twisted out of shape, crushed, and filthy, none of them could tell what animal it was—violence had reshaped it into something new, something disturbingly abstract.

Brian reached into a pocket and withdrew his utility knife. Geoff held up one hand and gave his head a gentle shake. No need to blunt the blade, he relayed without words. To demonstrate, he simply pulled one of the creature's extremities. It came away without effort, trailing limp sinew, a trickle of dark fluid, and a single bloated maggot. Katy grabbed it as soon as it struck the earth and slapped it into her mouth. It burst between her cavity-laden teeth, splattering her tongue with cold, vaguely nutty slime. She swallowed rapturously, eyes closed, face raised toward the perpetually clouded sky.

Geoff proffered the limb to Armaan who took it eagerly, gnawing at whatever remained of the rancid meat. Everyone received a similar portion and the following minutes were loud with chewing, retching, and the occasional sob. When the pilgrims finished their meager ration, they huddled together for warmth. Katy unwrapped the blanket she wore as a cloak and shared it with the others. It abraded their frostbitten skin and stank of the long journey, but they all welcomed the little comfort it provided.

Each sunk into a shallow half-dreaming state, recalling the

world as it had been before the bombs had fallen. But their dream-memories were half-formed, pocked with holes and shrouded in haze. The images and impressions were tantalizing, but heart-wrenchingly out of reach. It was almost worse than having no memory of the past at all. But that would hopefully change once they reached the movie palace. Survivors made the journey from all corners of the shattered world to see images flashing on the palace's movie screen—rare images of the world as it had been before, images without holes or an obscuring haze. The pilgrims hoped with every shred of their beings that it would reinvigorate their memories and give them the much-needed strength to persevere in this unimaginable hell. Having lost everything and everyone but each other, it was the only thing left that gave them reason to live.

Their breath clouded the air as they hovered between vaguely pleasant dreams and a waking nightmare. Armaan was the first to twitch awake. He moaned and burst into wheezing sobs. The din woke the others and they drew closer still, sharing his anguish. Geoff brushed the hair from Armaan's face in an almost maternal gesture and kissed the corner of his mouth, tasting tears, ash, and sour breath. Armaan moved into the kiss, opening his mouth, their tongues coated in putrescence. Joining in what had recently become a morale boosting ritual, Katy cupped Brian's cheek and pulled him toward her lips. Trembling hands explored the other's body; ribs, hips, and collarbones tangible through layers of fabric. The pilgrims traded affections: belts clattered, zippers growled, skin slapped weakly against skin. Focus on the electric rub of flesh on flesh. The internal warmth of the body. Your partner's breath against your neck. Drown out the fear. We can't lose hope now—these statements passed through each of their minds as they brought the other to passionless, anemic climax.

———

ONCE FINISHED, they lay together, shivering and exhausted under Katy's blanket. The wind lamented and in the distance, gunfire sounded. Muzzle flashes pulsed in the dust clouds smothering the highway. The display was perversely lulling, and soon the pilgrims succumbed to fitful sleep. This time, however, their dreams did not reach into a half-forgotten past, but rather centered on a single, shared image: a vast, reflective eye watching them from above. Or at least that is what they believed before they were struck by a bolt of lucid epiphany. It wasn't an eye at all, but a camera lens—though they could not discern who or what stood behind the apparatus. The camera hovered over their sleeping bodies, whirring mechanically, panning left and right with porno-graphic zeal. The air was filled with squelching, ripping sounds, and choked with the damp stench of the slaughterhouse.

When the pilgrims awoke, their mouths were full of blood, flesh was caught between their teeth, and one of their own was dead.

2

GEOFF HAD BEEN MUTILATED beyond recognition. Skull smashed, the contents fanned out in a crown of white, raw pink, and shimmering crimson. Among the detritus, several teeth and a single bloodshot eye were visible. It stared into an imprecise distance, seeing nothing. A fly crawled across the lead-grey iris. His body was likewise deformed. The chest had been crushed inward, near the sternum; stomach ripped open, loops of intestines trailing between his legs. His penis had been sawed off with a jagged instrument—probably a chunk of asphalt based on the black grit in the stump. Human teeth marks covered most of his body, and the muscles on his thighs and biceps had been stripped from the bone—likely eaten.

The pilgrims exchanged appalled glances. Blood covered their faces, chests, and hands. It had dried to a tacky reddish brown film. Unable to consider the implications of this tableau, Armaan grabbed his clothes and pulled them over his exposed skin, screaming all the while. His coat had been so heavily saturated with blood it froze into a bizarre, crumpled sculpture. He struck it against the ground to loosen the fabric, clumsily put it on. Following his lead, Brian and Katy grabbed their frosted garments and dressed.

"What happened?" Katy wailed. "What did we do?"

"It was a dream. We're still dreaming," Brian ranted.

"It couldn't have been us," Armaan said. He glanced toward the ruined gas station, stabbed a finger toward its blackest recess. "It was something in there." When he spoke again, his tone was low, almost a whisper. "The Carolith."

"Maybe they made us do it. They can do that, can't they?" Katy was sobbing, tears slicing tracks through the blood congealed on her face.

Brian simply stared at the corpse, reached numb fingers to his lips, his stomach. The fingers sank lower and he did something he had not done since childhood—he slipped one hand down the front of his pants and cupped his genitals. It was a nervous tick, a coping mechanism, totally unconscious until parents and schoolteachers told him to stop. He remembered their scolding tones as he followed the loops of Geoff's intestines with his eyes. A thin, white sheet of frost had formed over the corrugated flesh, giving it a surreal, artificial appearance.

"We can't stay here," Armaan said. "We're too close now."

"We need to bring him with us." Katy wailed, her words nearly incomprehensible.

"We already are," Brian spoke finally, his tone flat.

He turned and vomited his share of Geoff into the dirt. Blood, bits of masticated skin, and even hair was blended with the meager acid from his stomach. As soon as he was empty, the tears came, hot and stinging. He was not certain if they were the result of Geoff's passing, or the fact that he had just lost valuable, life saving calories.

"Fuck this," Armaan said. He grabbed Geoff's backpack, threw it over one shoulder. "Are you two coming, or am I leaving you here?"

Brian, hunched forward with his hands on his knees, spat, said weakly, "I'm coming."

Katy, still sobbing, shuffled over to Armaan and curled into his chest. He wrapped his free arm around her back, squeezed her against his body.

"We need to wash him off," Brian said, straightening.

Armaan considered the suggestion as he stared into Brian's cannibal mask. He shook his head. "Think of it as camouflage. Geoff can still protect us as we move deeper into the city. It'll only get more dangerous from here."

Brian groaned and Armaan thought he was going to throw up again, but he only leaned forward and let another glob of spit fall. When he moved closer to his companions, he gave Geoff's remains a wide berth. Armaan touched his face, trying to convey comfort with a glance, but realized the effect was probably lost through the layers of blood. He turned his attention instead over Brian's shoulder—at the wreckage of the gas station.

The darkness under the canopy shifted, seemed to breathe. For an instant, Armaan thought he could make out a vaguely human silhouette, black against black. And was that the whirring of an ancient camera? He pulled his gaze away.

"We need to get moving."

———

THE PILGRIMS TRUDGED DEEPER into the city, silent and guarded. As they neared the crippled skyscrapers of the financial district, they encountered the first people since leaving their tent city, three weeks ago. Travelers, like themselves, congregated toward the ruins, while others moved away, pulling makeshift rickshaws in quest of salvage. Every face was lined with misery; some were hidden under layers of filthy, bloodstained bandages; others had been distorted by some form of leprosy or cancer, skin turned a lumpy, ashen grey, hair missing save for the stray, bleached strand. Those who acknowledged the pilgrims swiftly looked away, those who did not gave them a respectable—or perhaps fearful—distance.

As they approached a collapsed, once-elevated highway, they encountered a disturbing scene. An uncountable number of bodies lined the pavement. Spools of nitrate film, partially burnt, had been threaded through their orifices, winding from anus to orbital socket, mouth to ear canal. The corpses were naked. On every stomach a different symbol was carved deep into the flesh —deep enough to expose the yellow layer of fatty tissue. The pilgrims did not recognize the symbols—they were unspeakably alien, a maze of twisting lines, dashes and curls. The only recurrent element was a single spiral tucked away somewhere in every etching. As Brian leaned forward to inspect the nitrate, Armaan grabbed his bicep and pulled him back.

"Don't look at it," he said. "It's not for us."

Armaan imagined holding the nitrate to the sky, seeing the images burned there, and screaming until he gargled blood and his carotid burst from the strain. For he knew not all films in this fallen world were considered equal. The symbols had made it apparent to him this gruesome scene was not the work of other humans, but the Carolith.

After the bombs fell, the Carolith emerged from the ruins and appropriated human art as their chosen form of expression, or perhaps communication. Their work appeared across the blasted landscape, and the theme was always the same: a marriage between filmmaking equipment and the human body. Though their method was apparent, the meaning behind these displays eluded the survivors. Armaan wondered whether these installations—celluloid threaded through flesh and processed with blood—were a method for the Carolith to consume cinematic media. As the thought entered his mind, he nearly burst into a fit of unhinged laughter. Before that could transpire, however, he dug his nails into his arm until he drew blood.

Brian looked at Armaan then back at the bodies. He stepped away. Katy moved beside him, arms wrapped around her chest. "There aren't any flies," she said, voice flattened by shock.

She was right. The bodies, aside from the carved symbols, were devoid of filth or signs of putrefaction. Where the pilgrims expected to hear buzzing, there was only the howl of the wind.

Acting on a hunch, Armaan scanned the perimeter of the installation. About ten paces from the furthest corpse was a strip of earth darker than the surrounding ruins. It curved into the distance, and veered behind the pilgrims, forming a circle around the installation.

Armaan approached, lowered on one knee. At first, his mind did not register what he was seeing, but when he focused harder he realized the circle was formed of dead flies. Thousands of them, their bodies rigid and undamaged as though they had simply been struck dead within a few feet of the installation. Their wings glinted in the meager sunlight.

A chill of dread passed through Armaan's body. He stood up and approached his companions, head on a swivel. "Let's go. Now."

3

WITHIN THE DOWNTOWN CORE, there were no roads to speak of, only loose pathways in and around the rubble. Survivors had established makeshift dwellings within the ruins, practically honeycombed one on top of the other. Only glimpses of them could be seen: the pale outline of a face, a toothless smile; the animalistic flash of fear-maddened eyes. The pilgrims did their best to ignore them as they moved closer to the movie palace.

Gone was the omnipresent dirge of the wind. In its place, the air rang with a chorus of screams and the occasional detonation of a makeshift bomb. The city had long become a battleground between various factions competing for resources and territory. Within the tent city, where the pilgrims called home, these conflicts were nothing more than hearsay, whispers. Now, the true scale and barbarism of these skirmishes were made plain to the outsiders. They were forced to use narrow tunnels and half-collapsed alleyways to circumvent the bloodshed. Combatants arrayed with makeshift armor—tire rubber, broken pieces of plywood, and metal siding—charged past the pilgrims, brandishing spears, bricks, machetes, and baseball bats studded with nails.

When they emerged from a particularly claustrophobic alley, the pilgrims encountered a second class of soldier. These were either completely nude—their bodies war-painted with ash—or clad in mail constructed with heavy scales of asphalt. Their breastplates were adorned with the cryptic emblem of the Carolith, spray-painted on or rubbed in with human waste. As the pilgrims scuttled across a collapsed bridge, one the nude fighters ran past them and into a crowd of waiting spearmen. The second he was impaled, the black device in his hand exploded, drowning the spearmen in a cloud of black smoke and a shower of blood.

Less than a block from the combat area, a building stood erroneously against a panorama of ruin. It was an imposing construction of red brick, with gargoyles perched on the corners of the roof. The marquis curved in a half circle around the face of the structure, the surviving letters suspended at odd angles, spelling nothing. A neon sign rose vertically from the center of the marquis. It was broken and the proprietors had tangled three flayed bodies through the lifeless glass tubing, as though to give the façade a touch of color, a sensational lure. Their mouths were frozen into horrified death screams. The pilgrims stopped and gaped at the structure, tears in their eyes.

At long last, their pilgrimage was complete.

————

THE TICKET BOOTH was blacked out with dust and dirt. Through the receiving window peered a face so altered by deformity it hardly looked like a face at all. Tumors sagged down the forehead and left cheek, obscuring one eye, while the other bulged from its socket, the white turned yellow by illness. The lips had been chewed away, leaving nothing but a layer of pinkish scar tissue. The gums were black and receded, the teeth abnormally long, thin, and exposed at the root. The nose was missing, the nasal cavity stuffed with a dirty rag.

"How many of you?" His visible eye darted over the pilgrims, but judging by his question he saw little or nothing. When the pilgrims were too stunned by shock and exhaustion to answer, he asked again, this time in a keening hiss, "How. Many. Of. You?"

Armaan took a tentative step forward. "Four," he said. Then quickly corrected himself, "Three. There are three of us."

The disfigured attendant shuffled around inside his booth. A moment later, a hand—callused, filth-encrusted but lacking deformity—emerged from the window holding three admission tickets. Armaan took them and handed one to Katy and Brian. The pilgrims stared in wonder at the pieces of cardboard. They were pristine, unbent, as though they had been printed that same day. Armaan raised the ticket to his nose and inhaled. The scent of fresh paper rushed directly to the pleasure centers of his brain. How long had been since he touched, smelled something new?

"Go inside. Show your tickets to the ticket taker," the attendant wheezed. "Don't just stand there. Tonight's an important night. Once the doors are closed, they're closed."

Armaan took Brian's hand, and Brian took Katy's hand, and together they entered the movie palace. The lobby was grand, baroque. A vaulted ceiling adorned with decorative plaster and copper filigree. A massive chandelier hung crooked from within a spiral of plasterwork, its prisms trailing clods of dust and ash so that it looked like the strung up carcass of something long dead—something that had been dragged from unimaginable oceanic depths.

Dozens of pilgrims, young and old, were scattered about the space, huddled against the walls, lying across the floor. Each bore some mark of their travels: scars, still-bleeding wounds, broken limbs, or the hint of a wasting disease; some stared in dumb wonder at their surroundings—tears glazing their eyes—while others slept or rocked back and forth, muttering to themselves. Despite the air of suffering, there was an almost tangible aura of anticipation crackling through the crowd—a collective bated breath.

Still hand-in-hand, the three pilgrims carefully picked their way through the supine bodies, searching for the ticket taker. As their gazes roved about the room, they noticed a banner strung over the archway leading to what they assumed to be the auditorium. It had been stitched together with miscellaneous scraps of fabric and old clothes. Smeared in umber paint were the words: WELCOME TO NOSTALGIA NIGHT.

Katy squeezed the hands of her companions. "We're in the dream, now," she whispered. "We won't have to close our eyes anymore. We'll see everything."

As they continued to stare at the banner like parishioners admiring a holy effigy, a woman in an immaculate blue uniform carefully maneuvered toward the pilgrims. She was smiling with her teeth and her cheap blonde wig was obviously askew, nearly covering one ear. Something black and glossy—visible only in fleeting glimpses—moved sluggishly underneath, and the movements coincided with the frantic darting of her eyes. She stopped a few paces in front of the pilgrims, and her mouth abruptly snapped open. The same dark substance glinted inside, in place of a tongue.

"Hello," she said. Her voice was recognizably human, but somehow incompatible with the body it issued from, as though she were overdubbed. "Thank you for coming to Nostalgia Night. Can I have your tickets please?"

The pilgrims reluctantly held out their tickets, and Katy remembered something one of the residents of the tent village had told her—some believed the Carolith used human hosts to "come through to our side". Animals didn't work; their minds and bodies weren't corrupted like those of the human race. "It's not even right to call us animals," the resident had said through missing teeth. "We lost that privilege the second we split the atom."

Still grinning, the woman received each of their tickets and slid them into a pocket at the front of her uniform. "We're about to let the patrons inside. Refreshments will be provided once you are seated. We hope you enjoy the show and thank you for making the journey."

. . .

4

THE AUDITORIUM WAS vast and cavernous. Long before the fifty-foot screen had been installed within the proscenium arch, the space had accommodated traditional theatrical performances. The boxes, gallery and wine-red curtain remained. Cherubs and satyrs leered from the yellowed plaster, mouths frozen in ignorant smiles. The seats were plush, but comfortable and the air was thick with the odors of popcorn and damp carpet. The pilgrims were astonished to breathe something other than blood or decay. But what surprised them even more was the complete lack of destruction. Even though the building was over a hundred years old—and within the radius of ground zero—it was impeccably preserved. Save for the occasional water stain, it was as though the palace had been cast in amber.

The pilgrims were seated in the middle row, centered with the screen. A little less half the roughly five hundred seats were occupied, and every patron had been given a tin can filled with stale, butter-soaked popcorn. Or at least, most of them thought it was butter—but examining it more closely, Armaan knew better. Before arriving at the tent village, he'd travelled with a man who called himself Pluto. While taking shelter in a deserted auto repair shop, Pluto had found a corpse in a utility cupboard. It was curled in the fetal position, as though in death it had hoped to be reborn. He'd dragged it out, and without preamble carved into the flesh with a rusty screwdriver. Holding out a flap of pale, jelly-like tissue to Armaan, he said, "We'll find a way to boil this down." And his lips peeled his lips back in a self-satisfied grin.

Bubbling in an oil pan over the fire, the smell was like frying bacon, and when Armaan peered inside the resulting slurry had the same color and consistency as the fluid glistening over their popcorn. Despite this realization, Armaan still placed a few popped kernels on his tongue. A blend of salt and fat sent his taste buds into a kind of shock—his palate had lost all standards and this sudden assault of familiar, junk food bliss, was almost too much to handle. He shivered, a quiet giggle rising in his throat. Peripherally, he considered the food might be drugged, but in his ecstasy, he failed to care.

Brian looked at him, rendered human fat shining on his lips. "It's good," he said and gave a short, vulnerable laugh. "I almost can't believe it."

Katy leaned forward in her seat to look at them. "I know. I didn't think I'd ever say this—not after everything that happened—but I think I'm *actually* happy." She gave a guilty chuckle and ran her palms over the hand rests, the can balanced on her lap. "In this place, I can almost imagine everything is back the way it should be. Sitting in a theater with your friends, eating, *enjoying* ourselves."

Armaan nodded and glanced at his popcorn. The illusion was not as ironclad as Katy suggested, there were holes: the rendered human fat, Geoff's blood on their faces, row upon row filled with the diseased, the dying, the psychotic—not to mention the inhuman proprietors of this establishment, the architects of this porous illusion.

The lights started to go down and the crowd gasped in one voice. The pilgrims gripped the other's clammy hand, squeezing in anticipation. The screen flickered and a series of symbols appeared. The trio recognized them from the art display under the raised highway: the runes of the Carolith. Armaan averted his gaze toward the floor and whispered for the others to do the same. Around them, patrons screamed, while others spoke in a rapid, unintelligible tongue. The energy in the space grew fanatical, a congregation of the bloodthirsty, the insane. It was clear to the pilgrims that not everyone in attendance was here to reinvigorate their memory.

The symbols stopped flickering. The pilgrims turned their attention back to the screen, the auditorium a firmament of darkness around them. The manic energy died as swiftly as it was born. Whispers and the restless creak of chairs echoed in the void. A title appeared against a black background: HOME-

SICK. A couple spectators shrieked in excitement. Someone clapped.

FADE IN:

INT. BEDROOM – DAY

A man lies on a bed, stomach to the mattress, his wrists and ankles bound together. To the extreme left of the frame—facing the man from behind—stands a second performer in a black ski mask. He is of average build; wearing a t-shirt and track pants that are too short in the leg, revealing hairy white ankles. In one hand, he holds a large carving knife.

He moves to the bed, braces his hand against the man's backside, and plunges the knife into his lower back. The man must be drugged, because it takes him several seconds to realize what is happening. He simply glances over his shoulder, as though someone had tapped him on the back. Only when ski mask pulls the blade out and stabs him again, does the man scream.

The pilgrims stared unflinchingly at the screen, but none of them focused on the bloodshed. Instead, their attention was riveted on the lone window visible in the frame. Though the video quality was poor, it was possible to distinguish the emerald etching of trees against a backdrop of clear, unblemished blue. It was morning, or early afternoon, and a slight swaying motion—a rearranging of pixels the size of bricks—suggested the presence of a breeze.

It was a strange experience to see such beauty after a seeming eternity in hell. The pilgrim's minds, dulled from trauma and the horrific monotony of the landscape, abruptly flared into new life, flowers blooming from a corpse. Katy recalled a summer with her family, when they stayed at her uncle's cottage in the country. She sat on the shore of the stream behind the property, dipping her toes in the water, watching the sunlight dance across its surface. Birds sang. Her mother laughed from the porch. A blue jay regarded her from its perch across the stream. She smiled at it, and whether inspired by the beauty of her surroundings or the slight buzz from her margarita, she imagined it smiled back with its dark, reflective eyes.

Now, sitting in the theater, she smiled and tears spilled down her cheeks.

Beside her, Brian cast his mind back to his childhood. He was playing in the park with his sister while their mother watched from a nearby bench. It was summer and both he and his sister were sweating from their game of tag. She was in close pursuit, hurling taunts and playful insults at his back, when she tripped over an exposed root and sprawled into the grass. Their mother stood and walked over, helping his sister to her feet, brushing the grass from her knees, the tears from her cheeks. It's okay, his mother said, you're okay. And she was. Brian recalled being so touched by his mother's cool-headed kindness, he approached and wrapped his arms around her. She smelled like the sun and clean laundry. In her embrace, he knew he was invulnerable to harm, that she could make all his pain and fear go away.

Armaan invoked a memory of when he attended university. It was Friday and he walked from his apartment to the house his best friend shared with two other roommates. They set up a foldout table and played beer pong until the sun was nearly extinguished and they were stumbling around, laughing from the alcohol. Later, more people arrived and the party grew so raucous the police were summoned. Seeing the red and blue lights reflected on the side of the house, Armaan grabbed the hand of the woman he'd been speaking to and made a mad dash for the baseball field behind the property. Once there, they bent over, hands on knees, and simultaneously laughed and gasped for air. The two of them—only having met that night—would become close friend throughout the duration of university.

Onscreen, the man on the bed screams. It's high and keening, more animal than human. Ski mask rolls him onto his back and plunges the blade into his stomach. The bed sheets transmute from slate grey to blackish red. The clip ends as ski mask pulls out a small handgun and shoots the man six times in the face. A close-up of the aftermath reveals a confusion of flesh and bone, a vague approximation of a mouth opening and closing like a beached fish. The camera pans again, catching a final glimpse of the window before slamming to black.

The pilgrims blinked like they had emerged from a dream.

They exchanged tearful, smiling glances, feeling as though part of their humanity had been restored. Their memories were more alive than ever, encroaching on the black coagulation of fear polluting their minds. The audience around them was animated, cheering, blubbering, and moaning in what could have been terror or ecstasy. Drunk from nostalgia, Katy said, "I'm so happy we made the journey."

"Me too. Very much," Armaan said.

"I wish Brian were here."

They all nodded but said nothing, reluctant to disrupt their happiness.

Another title screen pulled their attention back toward the screen: LAMENT #6 – THE INDEBTED.

FADE IN:

EXT. CITY STREET – NIGHT

A man in an expensive suit, his tie askew, expression harried, is being pushed down a sidewalk at gunpoint by two aggressors in masks, while—presumably—the cameraman walks backwards in front of the the businessman. You can hear him laughing, the proximity of his face behind the camera turning the sound into a low, tectonic rumble.

BUSINESMAN: Please. Oh God. I'll get you the—

GUNMAN #1: It's not back at the storage facility, you lying motherfucker.

BUSINESS: I don't…I don't know why it isn't there. Someone must've taken it.

GUNMAN #2: You're lucky we're in the open. Otherwise I'd shoot you in the back.

CUT TO:

INT HOUSE – NIGHT

The house is lavish but covered, floor to ceiling, with plastic sheeting. A chandelier glows like a dying star under a warped window of plastic. The gunman throws the businessman on the floor as the cameraman jerkily sets the camera on a tripod, ensuring everything is in frame.

The other aggressor fires his weapon twice, taking out each of the businessman's kneecaps. His screams are so loud, so frantic, the speakers crackle with distortion. He rolls around on the plastic sheeting

as the man holsters his piece, picks up a crowbar and beats the busi-
nessman until his arms and chest bend out of shape.

As they watched, the pilgrims felt every blow in their teeth. They exchanged glances, confused. There was nothing for their memories to latch onto, only this sterile environment—splashes of red on white—and the all too familiar barrage of violence.

A few agonizing minutes later, the businessman is a bloody sprawl on the floor. One of the gunmen moves behind the camera and returns with a machete. With the assistance of his companion, he hacks at the businessman's neck—blood spurts, limbs twitch—until his head rolls away, jetting blood on the decapitator's shoes.

CUT TO…

An extreme close-up of the businessman's head: eyes wide and glazed, mouth hanging open, blood still trickling from his nostrils. Someone is holding it up as the camera operator walks backward, tracking the subject in slow motion. Eventually, they move outside and the camera pulls away from the disembodied head, revealing an expansive courtyard rimmed with cypress trees. The sun is a burnished medallion in a cradle of delicate clouds.

The pilgrims gasped.

The scene restored to Brian's mind the European trip he took with his now-deceased partner a year before the war. There had been a definite atmosphere of dread—every television in every coffee shop tuned to the news—but the couple still managed to enjoy their vacation. After all, it would likely be the last one they took in some time. War made recreational travel effectively impossible. And so, they spent most of their time outdoors—eschewing media exposure—visiting historic sites, hiking the countryside, dining on cobblestone patios.

On an exceptionally hot day, while sharing a bottle of ouzo, Brian stared across the table at his partner. Her face was streaked with sweat, her hair wild from the humidity. And he wondered whether she would take him seriously if he asked her to marry him. They had once agreed that marriage wasn't for them, but the world was changing so drastically and violently, what had once seemed frivolous now carried a new significance. Marriage—an overt display of their love—could be a warding flare in this ever-darkening world. He continued to stare until she smiled affectionately, somewhat awkwardly, and asked what was wrong...

Everything below her neck abruptly disappeared, her throat turning red and ragged. The face lost its familiar shape, the eyes going dull, the skin blossoming into a garden of blood and bruises. Cringing in his seat, Brian squeezed the armrests, nauseous and gasping for air.

Onscreen, the man holding the head throws it out in front of him and kicks it like a football. It doesn't go very far—maybe a couple feet —before connecting with the courtyard and bouncing, the blood-soaked hair undulating with anemone grace.

As Brian's recollections merged unpleasantly with the film, Armaan managed to see beyond the cruelty onscreen as he sank into his own memories. The courtyard brought to mind the patio behind his grandmother's home. As a boy, he spent his summers there, using chalk to draw mythical creatures on the sun-warmed stones. He imagined the ornate flowerpots scattered around the area were home to beings made of twigs that protected his grandmother from harm. He wished now they were real, watching over his companions. But all they had were the Carolith, cruel, unfathomable, and made not of wood, but shadows and cold, hard stone.

Finally, Katy's disappointment from earlier sloughed away, replaced by a deep, near delirious, flood of happiness. She laughed silently, tears sliding down her cheeks. The sky...the sky in the film was so blue, so clear. She would give anything to stand under its immensity once again. It reminded her of after-school soccer games, family barbecues, and the scent of campfire...but those impressions mutated as the screen faded to black. Soccer games became a masked man kicking a severed head, family barbecues a group of starving, walking corpses cooking one of their own over a gasoline fire. And the smell: rich, heady, sickeningly sweet like spitted pork. Her hands trembled and she dropped the tin of popcorn.

A flurry of segments followed, pulling the pilgrims in and out of their memories like a slow drowning, every gasp for breath

another precious scrap of something they had lost. Scenes of
meticulous animal slaughter precipitated memories of long lost
pets, their unfettered joy and innocence; a sequence featuring a
school shooting from the head-mounted-camera perspective of
the shooter prompted reminiscences of their high school years;
and a graphic sex murder made them reflect on the opiate pleasure of intimacy, of reckless love.

However, these vignettes were scraped from their minds
when a familiar landscape appeared onscreen—*a ruined gas
station in a valley of rubble, its canopy leaning to one side, harboring
shadows. The camera pans away from the ruins, focusing on a group of
figures huddled in the distance. It approaches, its movements oddly
smooth considering the uneven terrain. Closer now, the pilgrims come
into view—four of them—sharing a single blanket under the gunmetal
sky. And there is Geoff, alive, eye closed, blue lips moving in a dream.*

Brian, Katy, and Armaan inhaled sharply as a weight plunged
into their bowels. The nostalgic high they had been riding—
though gradually losing potency—finally dissipated, bleeding
the color and optimism from their reanimated memories. They
sank deeper into their seats and watched, silent and horrified,
like prisoners hearing a verdict of death by execution.

*The image onscreen jump cuts to a lower angle, the camera posi-
tioned on a flat surface. The pilgrims are framed in medium shot, and
in the background stands what could only be one of the Carolith. Slen-
der, impossibly tall, its body a single intricately carved and polished
pillar of obsidian. No limbs or extremities are visible, no visage upon
which to focus, though its gleaming surface seems to reflect—or emit
from within—various shapes and hues, like colored water swirling in a
glass bottle. The effect is both hypnotic and vaguely disturbing.*

(Here the audience screamed, convulsed, cheered.)

*In a series of stop motion cuts, the Carolith approaches the sleeping
pilgrims. A blur of motion around its base as a shape—indistinct and
spasmodically alive—twitches toward their wrinkling brows. Touching
everyone but Geoff. The moment it makes contact, they startle awake.
Another jump cut and the Carolith is gone, but the camera continues to
roll as Brian, Katy, and Armaan rise with the sluggish, heavy locomo-
tion of somnambulists.*

Brian automatically reaches into his discarded coat and removes his utility knife. He extracts the blade as his companions watch, grips the handle in a white-knuckle grip, and hesitates. As though receiving silent off-screen instructions, he passes the knife to Armaan—Brian's former lover—who raises it above his head. He blinks and stabs Geoff in the neck.

Geoff's eyes snap open. Confusion transmutes to terror. He coughs once; blood gouts from his lips and splashes his chin. Armaan removes the blade and stabs him again, this time in the face. Steel penetrates flesh and glances off his cheekbone, gouging his left eye. The orb bursts, gushing vitreous humor like a spontaneous flood of tears. He screams and Armaan responds by stabbing him a third time, in the chest. Brian and Katy descend upon him with fingers and teeth, widening his new orifices to reach the meat, the marrow. Geoff thrashes, squeals, and cries for his mother. The camera pulls in as Katy tears away the first hunk of flesh from his neck, chewing and swallowing with a kind of detached ecstasy. Her pupils are fully dilated and in their darkness shapes and colors churn, flicker.

Watching the screen, Katy touched her lips. Her tongue still carried the taste of Geoff's blood. The sensation was more vivid, more real, than any memory she had revisited that night. She knew then their quest to reclaim what they had lost had been in vain.

5

THE PILGRIMS WATCHED the remainder of the film in a fugue state. On the periphery of their awareness—like sounds heard outside a nightmare—a series of victims screamed and begged for their lives, flesh burst open with wet rending sounds, blood bubbled from lips and nostrils. The other patrons whooped and wept, the air thick with the stench of popcorn and human filth. But none of these impressions could fully penetrate the shock that had calcified in their minds.

Eventually, the screen cut to black and faded in a single credit: A FILM BY XIVXVIXVIIIXIV. The words and numerals flickered and transmuted into the familiar but illegible sigils of the Carolith, then vanished before the pilgrims could turn away. Darkness pulsed. Light stuttered from the projectionist's window. Nostalgia Night had come to an end.

The wall fixtures came on, orange and buzzing. The other patrons stood and meandered toward the exit, but the pilgrims remained seated. Their reinvigorated memories had long since perished, putrefied into grotesque mockeries of what they had lost. Now a ravenous emptiness tore through them, calling into question the purpose of their pilgrimage. Had it all been for nothing? The memories merely a cruel taste of what they would never have again? What happened now? They would have to make the long journey back to the tent city, minus one member of their party. A member they had murdered and eaten for the pleasure of an audience. When they tried to imagine nights on their lumpy, stained mattresses, their minds clawed at nothing but nightmares and a sense of having reached an existential dead end.

The pilgrimage had given them reason to endure. Or, at least, that is what they believed before reaching its practical conclusion. Had the venture been an elaborate ruse, a myth fashioned by the Carolith and transmitted from one gullible mouth to another? A trap laced with poisoned honey to lure the broken and desperate into a false sense of hope?

The revelation struck the pilgrims all at once. Armaan leaned forward with his head in his hands, the can rolling from his lap and spilling on the floor. Katy shook her head in small jerking motions, eyes glazed and remote. Brian cupped a hand over his mouth as though to catch a sob. He moaned, spraying his palm with saliva and pink mucus. In that interminable moment, the pilgrims forgot where they were. Who they were. The person beside them faded into abstraction, agony their only distinguishable feature. Every trace of humanity sloughed from their bones—personhood, memories—leaving nothing but isolated shells of misery. Psychological defenses erected over a lifetime abruptly shattered, flooding them with decades of repressed emotion.

Brian, Katy, and Armaan regressed into a vaguely newborn condition, curling into themselves, muscles twitching, tears gushing from their eyes, mouths open in silent, natal screams. Time lost all meaning, dissolving into an endless stretch of terror and confusion.

————

UNOBSERVED, the ticket taker entered the auditorium with the awkward, twitching gait of a puppet. She stood in front of the vacant grey screen, smiling idiotically. After a beat, her mouth clicked open, "Ladies and gentlemen, you are cordially invited to join the proprietors of this establishment in a private conference. If you will follow me, please."

The pilgrims jerked into silence. Anointed with sweat and tears—the afterbirth of misery—they opened like nascent flowers. Stood on unsteady legs. Without a word, they followed the ticket taker outside the auditorium, down a narrow hallway, up a set of carpeted stairs, through a nondescript steel door, and onto the roof. The sky yawned above them, dwarfing them, roiling, grey—pregnant with radioactive rain. The city sang its erratic pulse: a chorus of screams, explosions, and gunfire. The pilgrims paused for a second, stunned by this assault of sight and sound after their incubation inside the darkness of the theater.

The ticket taker slowed her pace, turned. "Follow me, please."

The pilgrim cocked their heads and resumed their march until they stood with their guide on the edge of the roof. A wall of concrete rose to mid-shin, and when the pilgrims leaned forward to peer beyond it, they immediately reeled backward, and everyone but Katy fell sprawling on the sharp gravel.

From the entrance, the building had appeared no more than three stories tall. Now, the view from the rooftop suggested they were an unimaginable distance from the ground. Ruined edifices were reduced to the size of matchbooks, warring soldiers scuttled like insects. And the sky was swarmed with the floating, vaguely cylindrical shapes of the Carolith. Their bodies flashed and glinted in an exchange only they understood. When the fallen pilgrims regained their footing, the Carolith drew nearer, moving through the atmosphere with liquid ease.

As they stood transfixed at the edge of the world, the pilgrims heard the whirring of ancient cameras, smelled the vinegary stench of nitrate film. Once again they were the subjects of ravenous lenses—nourishment for an insatiable, incomprehensible malice.

Not looking away from the Carolith, Katy whispered, "This isn't our world."

And in those few words, the others understood their memories would never be enough. The world to which they belonged no longer existed. The realm they now inhabited was something else entirely, a hellscape forged through ignorance and violence. Why had they not perished alongside the rest of humanity— those fortunate eighty-percent—why had they been chosen to bear witness to the fruits of nuclear folly? We do not deserve any of this, they thought.

Brian clasped Katy's hand and Katy clasped Armaan's hand and they each took a moment to gaze at one another, crystalize in their minds the vulnerability in their companion's faces, the familiar contours of their bodies—perhaps the only beauty that remained in the world. When they were satisfied, they smiled and nodded to one another, transmitting their own form of silent communication. It was time to wake from the nightmare…

Silently, they stepped over the edge…

———

FADE IN:

EXT. CITY - DAY

Still holding hands, the three friends plunge down the face of the building. The camera follows in a rapid glide, lower and lower, until the ground rises to meet the jumpers in a liquid explosion of red. The camera lingers as a gentle shower of blood rains over the human wreckage. Then everything goes still. We stare for several moments longer, until the camera gradually pulls in and we get a clear look at the fallen bodies. It is nearly impossible to distinguish where one body ends and another begins. The friends have been reduced to a collage of meat and bone. However, as the camera draws closer still, we see that their mouths are relatively undamaged, and hint at the presence of smiles—the subtle, innocent smiles of children in the thrall of a pleasant dream...

FADE TO BLACK

WHERE CARRION CRAWLS

SAM RICHARD

SHE SAYS, "NO!" and the assault begins immediately. The director leaves no second for a breath before the actor starts tearing at the actress' clothes in animalistic fury. Tension filled the air of the small theater, forcing Amber to retreat into herself, reliving far too many horrible memories to count. The stench of an old friend's breath as he groped her at a party; music leaking from a punk house basement as the touring band's drummer's pleading became coated in rage; a regular at her old serving job back home pinching her ass as she dropped drinks off at his table and her boss assuring her that it was okay because he, "spends a lot of money here"; near-constant comments on the streets from strangers about her body, some of them unsubtle in their threat. Too many moments, both small and large, to count. And all the people who wouldn't listen, who wouldn't believe her.

"Are you ok…" Ollie's words hung hard, broken only by the woman on screen's panicked cries. "I can turn it off. It's really no problem. I'm super sorry, like I said, I haven't seen this for over a decade and I absolutely do not remember this part."

"I think I'm ok," her eyes reflecting the misogynistic display in the darkness. Waiting a beat, Amber prayed for it to finish; prayed that the movie would go back to the effects-heavy '80s B-film fare that they were anticipating, but the assault continued. The cries continued, echoing in the small, empty theater.

"No, wait. Is that ok? Would you be ok if we stopped?" Her voice was meek, tiny. And she hated it.

"Of course! I'm really sorry! Like I said, I totally wouldn't have picked this if I remembered this part. We've got other options. Let me just go back to the projection booth and put something else on. I'm so fucking sorry," he said, fully out of the tiny cinema before Amber could reply. *Fuck fuck fuck fuck fuck*, running through his head as he climbed the narrow stair set to the tiny room.

Renting out The Perisphere Micro-Cinema had been Amber's idea. Something to break the monotony of seemingly never-ending pandemic quarantine. Ollie figured it would be out of their financial reach but given how desperate the local theaters were to recoup some money, they had all drastically slashed their prices for private viewings. A hundred and twenty bucks for eight hours of 'watch whatever you want, BYOB, just don't make a mess or break our shit' was too good of a deal to pass up, especially with how cooped up they were feeling, nearly a year into Covid-19.

A viewing of *The Demon Dead* at The Perisphere had been their third date, so it made all the sense in the world to find some comfort and fun there. Ollie was grateful to get out of the house and spend some time together watching movies and talking in a different environment, though being the only people in the theater was strange, apocalyptic even.

The projection booth was little bigger than a closet and stuffed with all manner of old equipment. The theater showed classic, cult, and newer movies on multiple formats, and the room held an old film projector and two digital projectors with computers hooked up to them, among other less identifiable machinery.

Ollie looked out the small booth window as he tried to stop the movie. Accidentally hitting pause, the film went silent, frozen on a single frame of sexualized terror. The reflection of the still shot in the window's glass was distorted and magnified in unsettling ways. The victim's look of fear was replaced with cruelty, the perpetrator's look of rage replaced with tranquility. Their bodies contorted into one bizarre, inhuman shape. A mass of flesh and muscle and bones and blood, swirling together in a protoplasmic nightmare.

A shiver cut through him.

Sweat dripped down the back of his neck, soaking into his shirt collar. Refocusing his eyes past the small pane of glass, the original image on screen slowed his increasing heart rate. Back to the assault in progress--rage and fear. Brushing off the unease, he cursed himself again for picking *Telekinetic Carnage* and hoped Amber was ok.

Throwing on *Bug Chasers from Below*, a mutual favorite, he headed out of the booth. The lobby was sparsely decorated with a few screen-printed posters from previous cult and art film showings; a bulletin board full of outdated film screenings, fliers for year-old punk shows, and gallery events hung on the far wall. A small replica model of the space station from Grabowski's masterpiece, *From the Stars* sat on a white pedestal, encased in a clear plexiglass box. The sound of rain gently echoed through the room.

It was more modern art museum than movie lobby.

The entrance doors were closed and locked, per the manager's instructions, but Ollie couldn't help but feel exposed. Given the lights and the reflection, he couldn't really see through the glass, but he knew that he was being stared at. Or rather, stared through. Like someone was just out of view, standing in the dense rain, observing him from across the street.

It sent a renewed chill down his spine.

Retreating from the lobby and back into the dark safety of the theater, and pushing the paranoia from his mind, *Bug Chasers* was in full force. It was strange to not have to awkwardly shuffle past other people or worry about being quiet. Taking full advantage of their solitude, Ollie spoke, "Looks like it's really starting to come down out there. You doing ok? Sorry, again…"

"Yeah. I'll be ok. It's really not your fault, you don't have anything to be sorry for. I'm ok. A little shook, but it's already starting to pass. Going with *Bug Chasers* is a great idea. Sorry...I just, sorry." Amber's voice trailed off for a second. Before Ollie could say anything, she spoke again, "On another note, do you want more beer?" She was holding two freshly opened Granpappy's Mountain Streak tallboys.

Ollie grabbed one and slammed into his seat, guilt growing in his stomach. "I...I'm really sorry."

Amber bristled at his words, "Look, Ollie, I'm gonna need you to not do that to me right now; don't make me sit here and comfort you. It's not about you..."

The words stood as a presence between them.

"You're right. I just want you to be ok."

The screams of a neighborhood of terrorized citizens filled the room as Ollie took a swig of beer. He could tell from the glint reflecting off Amber's eye that she was studying him.

It hadn't been a simple relationship, but it was theirs. A perfect mixture of grief, trauma, PTSD, and compassion came together into something nice and comfortable.

Dating a widower couldn't be easy, he often reminded himself. Sometimes his grief, and where it took him emotionally was all he had the bandwidth for; sometimes it took over his life and fogged up the rest of the house, leaving room for little else. He had to make sure that his issues didn't smother Amber and what she was going through. That his pain didn't erase hers.

It was complex, and it could be hard, but there were both there for it.

He just couldn't help but feel like an asshole for accidentally subjecting Amber to a movie with a rape scene. He breathed in and out, reminding himself of what she'd said. It wasn't about him. And he shouldn't make it about him. A familiar mixture of anger and a paralyzing force grew inside of him. The thought of someone hurting her--assaulting her--made him see red, but it had nowhere to go. He pushed it aside, once again reminding himself that centering himself in her trauma was an incredibly shitty thing to do. He breathed out hard.

The glint in her eye was unflinching. Amber continued to

look at him in the darkness for a moment before taking a long swig of mildly cool cheap beer. It was soothing in her throat.

Numbness wrapped around her like a shroud, less the alcohol and more the oddly familiar comfort of a near-hit with PTSD. Reflexively clutching her pocketknife, she hated that something as stupid as an old Z-grade film from the 80s could have that affect on her, but she tried to not be too hard on herself; everything else was fucked enough as it was, no need to drag herself through the mud for one more thing out of her control.

Bug Chasers flickered across her vision, but never really penetrated as she sat in her emotionally anesthetized state, her fingers squeezing the hand-warmed metal of the knife spine. It was one they had watched a lot over the few years they'd been dating. An old favorite from her childhood, having watched it with her father at a young age. She could spit line after line without breaking. The cheesy dialogue and overwrought performances seared into her brain from so many viewings. Occasionally, she would catch Ollie absently humming excerpts of the synth-heavy score while he was cooking or working on things around the house.

It was a source of comfort for them both.

But something was different this time. Amber forced her mind from its retreat and back to the film, making herself pay attention. The images were warped and distorted, like the screen itself was bowing out at a strange angle. It took her a moment to figure out what was happening.

Dense, murky liquid poured in through the quickly shredding PVC screen. The *Bug Chasers* actors and sets were lost in the darkness of rushing, noxious fluid. Pounding rain and sloshing water echoed through the small theater, drowning out Amber's thoughts. Ollie was staring slack-jawed and wide-eyed at the coming tide of ooze. On purely animal instince, Amber jumped up, grabbed him, and pulled him out of the theater.

The lobby wasn't much better. Cloudy green-brown fluid was rushing under the front door like blood hemorrhaging from an exit wound. The white floor of the lobby was quickly going dark. A wall of murky liquid was crashing against the other side of the glass entrance door, which threatened to shatter under the pressure.

With few options, Ollie awkwardly pushed Amber up the rickety ladder leading to the projector room and slammed the small door behind them. Through the projection window, they could see the theater slowly filling with ooze, the flow having slowed down some after the initial rush.

Amber's eyes were drawn to the reflection in the glass. The actors in *Bug Chasers* were distorted and wrong, their bodies commingling in unnatural and obscene ways. Frantic, panicked smiles were on their faces. She recognized the scene, it was when the team of plucky neighbors first band together to fight the subterranean menace. Only this was different. Wrong.

They weren't assembling makeshift weapons and explosives in a musical montage set to cheesy new-wave. They were one singular organism of writhing cadavers and tearing flesh. Shattered bones were jutting out of the corporeal mass, muscle stretched beyond imagination, organs were discarded by some interwoven hordes and taken up by others.

Focusing her eyes beyond the glass, onto the slowing flood of ooze, the figures on the film remained the same. Twisted, tormented, broken, and reconstructed in bizarre formations. They danced with the rhythm of the fetid fluid like it was mutating them. A perverse transubstantiation of their recorded image. Their bodies, contorting into one unnatural entity.

———

SOMETHING MOVED IN THE BASEMENT. Harold hated that his eyes reflexively opened at the sound. All he wanted was sleep. He hoped Nancy hadn't woken up and did his best to get out of bed as quietly as possible. *Probably just a damn squirrel that got in again*, he thought to himself, hoping it was true.

His knees creaked as he stood, arthritic pain shooting up his legs. *Fuck getting old.* He wondered how much longer they'd both stick around. Nancy hadn't been in a good place in years, oxygen tank at her side most of the time. That the house was falling down around them certainly didn't help. Nor did her hoarding.

Harold had done what he could to keep the horde at bay from their bedroom, drawing a firm line in the sand. With her condition worsening, she hadn't been able to go out as much, so that certainly helped slow things down, but it didn't make the rest of their house any more livable given how long it had gone on.

Watching her struggle with her tank through narrow paths forged in an ocean of useless shit broke his heart. But it also made him angry. Angry at her for doing this to them, angry at himself for not seeing that it was a problem until it was far too late. No. For not admitting that it was a problem until it was far too late.

He hated himself for it. He had failed them both.

Through the labyrinthian halls of the horde he walked, careful to not brush up against anything that might make a sound. If it was an intruder, *and let's hope it's not*, he at least hoped he could get the drop on them before they could do anything; maybe he could startle them into running. *Probably just squirrels, or worse yet, rats*, he assured himself.

The house had gone eerily quiet since the initial sound had woken him, though the horde often worked as a sound dampener, with the dense walls of moldering clothes and newspapers and other assorted garbage.

In the dark of the night, the weight of it all grasped at his heart with sharpened fingers. It made him want to break down and cry. It made him want to scream. He did neither. Just another moment of weakness pushed down into his stomach. Just another feeling suppressed. He heard the ghost of his father's voice in the back of his head, from when he was 8 and fell off a ladder while trying to help paint their house, "Men don't cry, son…"

The words of a ghost; and one that he imagined he'd be meeting soon.

When he reached the back of the house and made his way into the kitchen, Harold thought that maybe he had imagined the whole thing, maybe he had woken himself up with a cough. But standing at the closed door to the basement, dull, wet noises were coming from the other side. Gently turning the knob, he held his breath as the door creaked open.

With no sudden movements or sounds from below, he started his slow descent along the narrow path of the squeaking wooden stairs. Harold's nose had stopped smelling the slow rot of paper, fabric, and wood long ago. He'd become immune to the piles of mouse droppings or how their dead stank as they secretly mummified beneath piles of trash.

None of that prepared him for the staggering, violent smell that met him about halfway down the stairs. It nearly knocked the wind out of him. It blinded his eyes and left him to pause with a coughing fit. The sloshing was more intense for a moment, before it went quiet.

The old wood creaked beneath him as he descended. In the darkness, he expected his foot to meet another stair but instead stinging liquid enveloped it, quickly soaking through his slipper and burning the flesh of his foot.

Pulling back, trying his best to run up the steps, his slipper crumbled away with each awkward step and there was something stuck to the bottom of his blistering sole. Staggering upward, a rush of fetid liquid followed him, splashing against the basement door as he slammed it closed.

The impacts didn't stop. Over and over again, shockwaves from the thing on the other side. He'd tumbled onto his ass as he'd closed the door in a panic, his injured foot having slid out from under him.

Pain overwhelmed his fear of whatever was on the other side of the door. Looking down at his engorged foot, nothing made physical sense. His anxious mind struggled for a moment to comprehend what he was looking at.

A rat was stuck to his sole.

Its innards were gushing out of the mouth, a thin line of blood trailed behind Harold's movements. He couldn't wrap his mind around the poor, smashed creature. How was it stuck to him?

Trying to tear it off sent blinding pain up his leg. The thing on the other side of the door continued to pound but it was all background noise to the anguish.

Where his flesh and the rat connected was covered in dark boils and blisters; flecks of blue and white peppered the swollen tissue. Harold's foot was quickly turning crimson and a wave of panic flooded his brain. Without thinking, he crawled over to the countertop and grabbed a chef's knife from the knife block. Pushing the tip of the shimmering blade between his sole and the decaying creature, several of the blisters audibly burst, oozing red-black liquid. A mixture of blood, and puss pooled on the linoleum beneath him, soaking into his pajama pants.

The pain was unreal. But he pushed through, tears streaming down his cheeks. His breathing was labored, and he thought he might have a stroke, but Harold kept cutting. A few times the blade dug too deeply into the meat of his foot and hit bone, forcing him to backtrack. Finding the spot where he and the rodent met was the real challenge.

Slowly, he filleted the rat from his sole inch by inch. The lake of gore beneath him widened, running along the floor towards the basement door, towards the mass still slamming against the other side. For a brief moment, Harold wondered what would happen if his blood made contact with the thing, but pain over-shadowed his thoughts as the rat flopped down towards the floor under its own weight, stretching and tearing at the remaining skin it was still tethered to.

In one swift movement, Harold pulled at the rat, trying to tear it clean from his mangled foot. It gave, but chunks of flesh and tissue came with it, leaving a crater in the bottom of his heel. More blood poured out of it, this time it was fresh and vibrant, not the fetid, puss-filled blood from before. Clean, healthy blood.

Wrapping a dish towel around his foot, Harold tried to stand, but the world twisted and turned as he stood. Bracing himself against the counter, he waited for the room to right itself before he took off, back through the rat's nest of their house.

Blood seeped through his makeshift bandage, leaving a

streak of bright red blood trailing behind him. After a few steps navigating through the chaos, his bandage started picking things up. Old mail and moldering clothing affixed to the sopping fabric around his foot. It didn't help his hobble. Before he could clear the room and head upstairs, the basement door splintered open, sending chunks of sodden wood crashing onto the packed countertops.

It was coming.

Harold hurried his pace, his foot throbbing beneath his weight. Pushing against the makeshift walls of the horde, they shifted under the pressure, threatening to topple over him. There was no time to think, no time to be careful. The mass was starting to ooze into the room behind him. The stench hit him first. But he also heard it.

Thousands of pounds of newspaper and old junkmail made a bizarre, expanding noise when they were reintroduced to moisture. He imagined the mummified rats and mice doing much the same. It sounded alive.

By the time he hit the stairs, the liquid was close, having enveloped much of the room behind him. *No real loss*, he couldn't help but think momentarily, before the panic flooded back as he ascended the cluttered staircase, the oozing mass filling in the gaps behind him.

Inside the bedroom, Harold tried to wake Nancy, but she wasn't responsive. The pills the doctor had given her worked a little too well this time of night and all she managed was a mild groan before she fell back into silence. Not even a flutter of the eyes.

The stench followed behind him, and Harold's mind raced at what he could do, how he could save her. How he could save them both.

His arthritic knees and shoulders were too far gone to be of any help. Not like he could pick her up and sling her over his shoulders like he had in the old days, back when things were better; before the horde and the creeping resentment. Before life had passed them both by.

There was no time to think. The thing was already oozing

through the door frame. Fuck the arthritis. Harold did his best to prop Nancy up, cradling her in his arms like he had walked into their honeymoon suite the day they'd gotten married. But she'd been so full of sass and vibrancy back then. Now she hung loose in his arms. Underweight and near lifeless. Her breathing gently fighting against his struggling biceps and forearms. His shoulders were on fire, the joints threatening to pop out of socket.

Carrying her to the far end of the room, he tried to place her gingerly on the floor but she slipped, crashing with a muted thud. No time to think. Tired hands prying at the window. The damn thing squealed like it had never been opened before, straining against layer after layer of ancient paint and swollen wood. By the time he turned back to grab her, it was too late. The mass had swallowed her feet, coating them in slime.

Stifling a scream, Harold tried his best to pick her up, but it was coming too quickly. First her shins, then her knees, then her thighs. He had to jump halfway out the window to avoid being consumed himself. Hanging half in and half out of a life he had begun to hate, Harold watched the only person he'd ever truly loved become one with the reeking organism.

She went peacefully, in that there was no struggle beyond a faint, slumbering whine, but tears burned his eyes as she was slowly overcome by the putrid ooze. Hanging out the window, the liquid swelled and grew, as if it was absorbing Nancy. His heart all but stopped beating, the weight of it all crashing down upon him, but the thing kept creeping ever closer despite his grief.

It crawled up the wall, swelling around him, threatening to either swallow him whole or push him out of the house. The liquid brushed against the hair on his leg, singeing it and adding a new layer to the cacophony of unpleasant odors. His skin screamed in anticipation of the coming pain.

Harold couldn't hold on any longer; couldn't choose between staying with Nancy, *Oh god please forgive me*, he cried over and over. *What have I done?*

There wasn't time for another thought. It was all happening

too fast. His grip slipped and out the window he went, praying for death--but not *that* death--crashing into the recycling containers and hitting the hard, wet pavement below. A fresh creak settled in his bones as he shook himself off and stood up, but he was intact. His foot was on fire, but that certainly wasn't new.

From below, he watched the house bloom with ooze. It poured out of every open window, and it crashed through the closed ones. Walking backward, away from the noxious fluid, Harold wept until he couldn't breathe. His tears met the rain and became one with the deluge.

Through hazy eyes he followed the mass as it rolled down his block, away from his neighborhood, and out into the city at large. Keeping his distance, he knew he would do anything to stop it, now that he knew what it was capable of.

As they went, he watched it enter random buildings and houses, growing in size as it poured out, having absorbed everything it needed before going onto the next victim. It seemed to operate more on instinct than logic, more animal than human, but certainly more alive than liquid should be.

The longer it went on, the more he allowed his anger to fester and grow. Nothing mattered now but stopping it, getting some kind of revenge. His relationship with Nancy hadn't been perfect, and lord knew he played a role in that, but that didn't mean he didn't love her. That didn't mean he didn't adore her. It just grew more difficult and complex as their lives went on. Ultimately, that's what he'd signed up for.

Initially, he cared less about the other people it would hurt, more about what it had done to him. It had rolled through houses full of unseen inhabitants. Anonymous, faceless, voiceless fodder. The occasional muffled scream began to tear into his soul, but he didn't know what to do.

Watching it roll into a tiny movie theater, leaving the rainswept street behind it, Harold stood in the downpour for a minute, wondering what he could even do to stop it. Wondering what he could do to stop it from consuming the man staring at him from the bright white lobby of the tiny movie theater. The first human face he'd seen since Nancy's.

———

A SMALL AMOUNT of fluid oozed in through the cracks in the door. Through the projection window, Amber and Ollie watched it slosh and rise in the theater. The liquid mass pulled in most of what it touched. Wood and some fabrics ended up in the slurry, but plastic-based things were left alone. Like it only wanted organic matter.

Amber screamed at Ollie to figure something out, but he sat there in a daze. Through slurred speech he spoke. "I had this dream once. It was fucked up...just like this..." before trailing off. She shouted louder, but his glassy eyes just stared out the tiny window, onto the growing pool of rotting slop.

"There's something in the center of it," he said, flatly.

Amber screamed. "It doesn't matter, we have to get the fuck out of here. Ollie! I need you to..." Her words were cut short by a hard impact and the cracking of glass as fluid slammed into the wall and the window.

Again. And again.

Glass shards shattered as they hit the ground. Dense, putrid air filled the small room, burning both of their eyes. The liquid poured into the projection booth, first as a trickle then as a flood, consuming all the organic materials it consumed. Absorbing them. Mutating and mutilating them.

But as quickly as the flood began, it slowed. A large mass blocked the window, jammed inside its small frame, reducing the flowing putrescence to a minor leak. As it dwindled, the form grew clearer. A corporeal form was before them, half in and half out of the small room.

A woman. Her tangled hair obscured her face, but her sagging, pallid skin showed only death.

Ollie's shock shook off and he reached for her, hoping to help her; hoping to end this nightmare. But something was off.

Her flesh was mangled and coated in slime, but below it was movement. He could hear it, sense it.

The back-pressure inched the woman further into the room, her flesh scraping off at the window frame, revealing flaking white muscle speckled with blue and black mold. It edged her closer to Ollie's hand, pressing his palm into her scalp.

A scream filled the booth and rang in Ollie's ears, wholly unaware that it was coming from his own mouth. Cold burning crawled through his hand and up his arm, like being stabbed with red hot knives. He tried to pull away, but he was stuck to her head.

The force of the yank shifted her weight, pulling her deeper through the window, bringing a fresh tide of fluid through with the movement. It also jostled her head and moved her hair, revealing a face covered in rows of clear, brown teeth forged from jagged fragments of broken bottles. Her empty eyes stared back at Ollie. Beneath the dark slime and her tattered clothes, something moved. Writhed.

Amber grabbed Ollie's forearm and tried to pry him free from his cranial shackles, but it wouldn't give. As she pulled, the woman came even further in the window, her flesh rolling back against the frame, like old paint being scraped away. The thing underneath undulated and squirmed as fluid began rushing into the room. Sloshing slop splashed Ollie's arms and face. His screams grew worse. Pulling Ollie onto the computer desk, Amber pushed down tears, unsure of what was even happening, of how this was happening.

Looking at the face of the strange woman he was tethered to, Ollie's panic recalled the coalescing bodies he'd seen reflected in the now shattered glass. The way it made him feel unnerved and disjointed. He wanted to recoil in horror, but his arm wouldn't budge. His hand wouldn't break free. The woman's hip bones were tearing into the wooden window frame. His skin was on fire. Bits of bone and filth and teeth and shards of wood splintered out of his flesh, where he'd been splashed.

The pain jolted through him with every movement. The

undulating under the woman's skin slowly pressed her through the window.

And then her eyes opened.

Moldy flecks scraped off as her eyelids fluttered, bluish white obscured her pupil, covering the entire iris. Her mouth opened, filling the room with a loud, multi-tonal whine. Fluid poured out of her gaping maw in uneven, lurching splashes, like a jug of wine held upside down. Ollie couldn't help but look deeper. Something was moving within. Amber screamed and tried to pull him away, but every tug brought the woman closer to them, further through the window. The fluid was halfway up the desk. And they had nowhere to go.

Tattered black fur flashed in the woman's open mouth and sickly sounds came out. Still staring, Ollie wrenched his hand, desperately trying to uncouple himself. The pull jostled the woman's chest against the old wooden desk they were standing on. Masses of fur and mold, black water and half-digested, reconfigured body parts poured out of her. The thing writhed on the floor.

Rats, organs, mold. They were as one.

Ollie saw stars and the pain in his hand swelled. His flesh was being severed, flayed and burning clenched his arm, all the way up to his shoulder. Amber hovered over him, cutting his hand free from the woman's head. Unbearable pain shot through him as Amber sliced him free, little by little. As he squirmed and moved, so did the woman. He screamed and on the final cut, a pocket of wet mold evacuated from her mouth, filling the room with an odorous mephitis. Ollie's eye rolled into the back of his head as the two were separated.

Amber grabbed Ollie, stopping him from falling to the floor, into the rising tide of slop, and held on for dear life, doing her best to press her face into his collarbone, hoping to not breathe in any of the hazy stench.

A light bloomed above and an arm reached down. Indecipherable shouting filled the room, but Amber couldn't understand. It was all just noise. Then a shaky wooden ladder dropped into the room, splashing in the slop. Pieces of wooden debris, body parts, and junk affixed themselves to the wood with muted cracking noises.

Slapping Ollie, Amber tried her best to pull him out of whatever state he was in, but it was no use. Suddenly there was an old man standing in front of her, one foot on the desk and the other on the ladder. "We need to go," is all he said, firmly.

Amber tugged at Ollie's cheeks and he came out of it, his eyes bouncing around in his head. Leading him to the man on the ladder, she did her best to position his hands on the rungs and pushed him up. He lackadaisically compiled, climbing the ladder as if he were sleepwalking or drugged.

As quickly as she could, Amber followed them, pushing Ollie up as she went. The ladder creaked and moaned under their weight, threatening to buckle, as the fluid rose to the top of the desk. Looking down, she saw the woman move. Her blank eyes stared at Amber with something approaching recognition. Above Amber there was a cracking sound and Ollie's weight shifted, pushing her towards the slop. Her feet threatened to fall into the murk. Then the splash came.

As did blistering pain on her face and neck.

Pushing back against Ollie's weight, she stabilized herself just in time to see the old man fighting for footing in the liquid. His face was covered in bits and debris, his arms glistening with slime, rats, and miscellaneous body parts.

And then he touched the woman.

They formed as one unit, one organism. His eyes pleading for Amber to help, but his throat giving nothing but a dull whine. Their two bodies merged, spreading a pool of dark, perfect red into the flowing water as they split apart and reconfigured themselves. Specks of blue and white mold growing on red boils and blisters where their flesh met. Bones cracked and muscles stretched until they were woven together.

A hand from above pulled Amber up. She was wholly unsure of what she was seeing, of what was happening or how it could happen, but she pushed herself up, following the guiding pull of the phantom arm.

She was lifted through a small hatch until she fell to the roof above the projection booth. Rain poured upon her and small black pebbles dug into her skin but the discomfort proved her reality; it proved that she was alive. That she wasn't dreaming.

Uncoupling from Ollie, who seemed less out of it, she struggled to think of anything to say, as much as she struggled to come up with what they should do next if that thing was still following them.

The familiar discomfort of shock wrapped her like a cloak and she gripped the blood-smeared knife in her pocket. Ollie stared at her. His face was soaking in the pouring rain. Opening his mouth to speak, nothing came out. Then he cleared his throat and tried again. This time a pool of dark fluid poured out of his mouth, meeting the collecting water at his feet.

A look of pain flashed across his eyes before they rolled into the back of his head, slowly returning with a vacant bluish white. The rising tide of liquid inside of the theater began to spill over the open hatch, out into the world that had briefly been their sanctuary.

White mold grew out of Ollie's mouth, spreading over his teeth and onto his lips.

Amber tried to run, but the flowing liquid was everywhere. The co-mingling bodies of the man and woman pushed through the hatch, riding on a wave of malodorous fluids.

Jumping to the lip of the roof, Amber looked down at the street to see dark liquid rolling under the splashing rain. Clumps of debris, animals, and human tissue writhed in the filth. Not in it. As part of it.

Crying, she sat on the edge of the theater roof, running her fingers over the spine of her knife. Her safety blanket. The first gift Ollie ever gave her. Clicking it open, she teased the razor-sharp blade, lightly dragging the pad of her thumb across it, letting it bite her ever so slightly. A small trickle of blood ran down her hand, soaking into her pants, quickly diluted by falling rain.

She figured that's what it would be like. Just becoming one with another thing. But time and time again this had happened when she hadn't wanted it to. She was done joining bodies she didn't pick. She was done being forced upon by others. In the reflection of her blade, the mass swelled behind her and the tattered bodies loomed over her. So she dragged her knife across her throat like she was cutting an errant stitch.

And it didn't feel good. She hated it, and the way tears streamed down her face and met the freshly opened wound, but it was her choice to make. No one else's.

STORY NOTES

The Watcher's Digest - Katy Michelle Quinn

I wrote this story near the beginning of the COVID-19 pandemic. I was thinking a lot about those public spaces that are approaching obsolescence, theaters included. I imagined a time when a modern theater would be a ruin. Ruins are intoxicating settings to me.

Once I had that, I sprinkled in some scifi elements I have developed for this and other stories: a near future where America has collapsed into problematic citystates, queer folks who are struggling against systems that prioritize the privileged, and some ooky cosmic horror to congeal it into a slimy whole. Thanks for reading!

A Marriage of Blood and Pus - Charles Austin Muir

Here's an idea: A Filipino guy breaks into an old porn theater and battles a succubus. Even better... a succubus from the myths of his own culture! You've got sleaze, nostalgia (porn on the big screen!), a supernatural villain, and a hero from a marginalized group, all in one story! Plus, your editor tells you there's no constraint on mood or theme. Do what thou wilt shall be the whole of the Law!

I figured I could knock the story out in eight weeks (I'm a slow writer). Eight months later, I'm just relieved I finished it and Sam thinks it's publishable. Honestly, it's the most personal thing I've ever written. You see, my wife was diagnosed with stage 4 colorectal cancer in 2019. I wanted to compose a tribute to her ability to endure in the guise of horror fiction. My mission became a test of my own ability to endure creatively... every word was a battle against demons I know must be pacing around inside me.

It didn't help that as soon as I started writing it, Kara's chemo side effects put us in the Emergency Room every few weeks through the winter. My post-surgical wound care skills quickly went from high school to master's degree level and I found myself living what I was writing, sort of. Maybe that's why I spent more time building the world of the story, because like the movie screen it highlights, my desktop monitor became a portal into my worst fears. I am honored that Sam let me explore my nightmares for some 12,000-odd words, and hopeful that if you made it out of the forest all right, you found something in them to enjoy.

The Reassigned - Jo Quenell

Sam asked me to write a fun movie theater horror story and instead I wrote something really upsetting and harsh. Oops. From the start I wanted to explore the trope of forced gender assignment in the vein of Sleepaway Camp or The Skin I Live In, filtered through a transgender perspective. But until I had a finished draft in my hands, I didn't expect the end result to be so ugly.

It took me forever to finish this story. I wasn't sure if it was something I was comfortable submitting. It's not the first thing I have written since I began transitioning, but it is easily the most personal. After reading a draft, my partner said it felt like I wrote a horror story for myself. I think that's true. This fucker contains a lot of my own fear and trauma. It reflects a lot on my relationship with internalized transphobia and misogyny; shit that haunts me no matter how far I stray from masculinity. Putting this intimate weight into a nasty, mean-spirited story felt intense, and at points I felt like a bad person for what I was writing. But that discomfort felt significant. I put more of myself into this story than any I've written before and it's important to share that, even if the end product paints a very bleak picture.

Thanks to Sam for once again seeing something in my writing worth pursuing. And thanks to all the wonderful trans people in my life, whose beauty and resilience make me feel inspired when the world gets harsh.

Nostalgia Night at the Snuff Palace - Brendan Vidito

Okay, bear with me here. I'm not used to sharing behind-the-scenes info about my stories…

When I was eleven, I had an appendectomy and was given morphine for the pain. I had an unexpectedly strong reaction to the drug. I remember opening my eyes to find a tall, narrow—almost cylindrical rock—standing at the foot of my bed. Apparently—according to my family—my eyes grew wide with terror. They asked me what was wrong, and in a voice laced with panic, I said, "There's a rock beside my bed." That morphine-induced image burned itself onto my brain, and I knew it was only a matter of time before I used it in one of my stories. The opportunity finally arose with "Nostalgia Night", and the interdimensional Carolith (a Latin portmanteaux translating to Flesh Rock/Stone) were born.

To be honest, I have very little memory of writing this piece. It was—as far as I can recall—the only story I wrote during the global shutdown. My mental health had been growing increasingly frayed in the months leading up to the pandemic, and the lockdown certainly didn't help matters. Whenever I managed to get some sleep, it was fraught with nightmares. And those nightmares kicked into overdrive one night after watching the 1984 TV movie *Threads*. For those unfamiliar, it's a disturbingly realistic account of a nuclear attack on the city of Sheffield in Northern England. It honestly fucked me up. I was still thinking about it days—no, scratch that—weeks after the credits rolled. So, when Sam approached me with idea for this anthology, the nuclear trauma of *Threads* flash-fused with my desire to write about the nostalgia for the cinema many of us were experiencing during the pandemic. The result, as you have seen, is one of my most unpleasant stories.

Reading it over, I can't help but notice my flat, disaffected approach to violence, and the somewhat saccharine descriptions used when describing the characters' memories. This was my attempt to contrast the two and illustrate just how mundane fear and brutality have become in this surreal, almost Boschian version of the apocalypse. But, more importantly, I wanted to frame the memories as a kind of beacon, demonstrating that no matter how horrendous the global situation, happiness can be found in smaller, seemingly trivial matters—a fond memory, a good book or movie, a smile from a friend or coworker. The world is a horrible, disgusting, cruel, and frustrating place, but if you know where to look, it can be pretty fucking cool sometimes. Trust me, I wrote a story about rock monsters, cannibalism, and snuff films. I know what I'm talking about.

Where Carrion Crawls - Sam Richard

I didn't intend to write a story with themes of sexual assault. Something I've gotten pretty decent at as a writer and widower is starting a story and realizing halfway through (or later even), that I'm actually processing a specific aspect of grief or trauma. It was something that came up a lot when I was writing the stories in *To Wallow in Ash & Other Sorrows*.

This was a little different though, how out of the gate the theme came. I had the idea of a couple renting out movie theater and some eco-horror aspects (given my love of the 80s *Blob* remake). But from the jump, the first line came out as it is now. And as I wrote, I realized how much of this story was me trying to process having so many loved ones who are survivors of sexual assault. How powerless it makes me feel. But also how I can't make their experiences and trauma about me. How I can't center myself in their pain.

As I wrote, the story also revealed itself to be about the way in which society literally shapes us and our relationships with each other; our relationships with ourselves. The way it takes from us, and manipulates us, and puts us back together in new and unhealthy ways.

So this thing that was supposed to be super fun 80's VHS b-grade horror got a lot darker and more personal. Which I think is what happened to all of us with this book. And given the state of the world right now, I'd say that's fair.

My main hope is that I handled this subject with the sensitivity required, that it doesn't feel exploitative or shitty. But this is something that I can't determine. It will be determined by you, the reader. Just know that this came from a place of compassion and pain.

CONTENT WARNINGS

The Watcher's Digest contains graphic eroticism and gore.

A Marriage of Blood and Pus contains pornographic content, violence, harm to animals, and graphic medical descriptions.

The Reassigned contains transmisogyny, transphobia, gendered violence, sexual assault, and discussion of gender confirmation surgery and procedures.

Nostalgia Night at the Snuff Palace contains gruesome depictions of violence, including suicide, cannibalism, and bodily—including genital—mutilation.

Where Carrion Crawls contains brief depictions of and discussion about sexual assault, portrayals of harm to animals, death, partner loss, trauma, bodily mutilation, and suicide.

ABOUT THE AUTHORS

CHARLES AUSTIN MUIR tells stories about blood, tumors, alternate realities, chaos magic, and that time he thought he was going to die in a porn theater. He is the author of *Slippery When Metastasized* and the Splatterpunk Award nominated *This Is a Horror Book*. His fiction has appeared in several anthologies, including *Peel Back the Skin*, *Year's Best Hardcore Horror Volume 1*, and *The New Flesh: A Literary Tribute to David Cronenberg*. A former cynophobe (someone afraid of things that go *woof*), he also runs Biggy Sancho Books, a micro-press dedicated to publishing doggy-themed kids' books by his wife, writer/illustrator Kara "Picante" Muir.

JO QUENELL is a transgender lady who lives in Washington State and writes. Her short fiction has been featured in various zines and anthologies including *Bleak Friday*, *LAZERMALL*, *Beautiful/Grotesque*, and *Teenage Grave*. She is the author of *The Mud Ballad*, released by Weirdpunk Books in May 2020. She teaches middle school, which is far more frightening than any work of fiction.

KATY MICHELLE QUINN is a queer transwoman who inhabits the forest of the Pacific Northwest with her partner and their cats. She has written two books: *Girl in the Walls* from CLASH Books and *Winnie* from Eraserhead Press.

SAM RICHARD is the author of *Sabbath of the Fox-Devils* and the Wonderland Award-Winning Collection *To Wallow in Ash & Other Sorrows*. As the owner of Weirdpunk Books, he has edited and co-edited several anthologies, including the Splatterpunk

Award-Nominated *The New Flesh: A Literary Tribute to David Cronenberg, Zombie Punks Fuck Off,* and *Beautiful/Grotesque.* Widowed in 2017, he slowly rots in Minneapolis.

BRENDAN VIDITO is the author of the Wonderland Award-winning collection of body horror stories, *Nightmares in Ecstasy* (Clash Books, 2018). His work has appeared in several anthologies and magazines including *Dark Moon Digest, Tragedy Queens: Stories Inspired by Lana Del Rey and Sylvia Plath,* and *Pluto in Furs.* He also co-edited the Splatterpunk Award-nominated anthology *The New Flesh: A Literary Tribute to David Cronenberg* (Weirdpunk Books, 2019) with Sam Richard. He lives in Ontario, and is hard at work on his first novel. You can visit him at brendanvidito.com, or follow him on social media.

To Offer Her Pleasure by Ali Seay

After the death of his father and his mother taking off, it becomes clear to Ben that the only thing he can count on, is no one to count on. Until he finds the book. One that calls forth a shadowy horned figure.

She comes with unexpected gifts and the comfort of a dependable presence. And she asks for very little in return, really. The more Ben offers her, the easier it gets.

Sometimes, family requires more than a little sacrifice…

Things Have Gotten Worse Since We Last Spoke by Eric LaRocca

Sadomasochism. Obsession. Death.

A whirlpool of darkness churns at the heart of a macabre ballet between two lonely young women in an internet chat room in the early 2000s--a darkness that threatens to forever transform them once they finally succumb to their most horrific desires.

What have you done today to deserve your eyes?

"A startling affair...I'll be cleaning up particles of darkness in my office for weeks."

— JOSH MALERMAN (*BIRD BOX, INSPECTION*)

She Who Rules the Dead by Maria Abrams

Henry has received a message: he needs to sacrifice five people to the demon that's been talking to him in his nightmares. He already has four, and number five, Claire, is currently bound in the back of his van.

Too bad Claire isn't exactly human.

"I fucking loved this book! Just when I thought I knew where it was headed--I was wrong. And I love to be wrong. A thrilling ride. I want more!"

— ALI SEAY (*GO DOWN HARD*)

Made in the USA
Monee, IL
09 June 2024

59148714R00090